THE UNSTOPPABLES
TEAM ONE

BOOK ONE

FURIED

USA TODAY BESTSELLING AUTHOR

HEATHER SLADE

fury

/ˈfyo͝orē/

one of the three goddesses of
punishment

MORE FROM AUTHOR HEATHER SLADE

BUTLER RANCH
Kade's Worth
Brodie's Promise
Maddox's Truce
Naughton's Secret
Mercer's Vow
Kade's Return
Butler Ranch Christmas

WICKED WINEMAKERS
FIRST LABEL
Brix's Bid
Ridge's Release
Press' Passion
Zin's Sins
Tryst's Temptation

WICKED WINEMAKERS
SECOND LABEL
Beau's Beloved
Coming Soon:
Cru's Crush
Bones' Bliss
Snapper's Seduction
Kick's Kiss

ROARING FORK RANCH
Coming Soon:
Roaring Fork Wrangler
Roaring Fork Roughstock
Roaring Fork Rockstar
Roaring Fork Rooker
Roaring Fork Bridger

THE ROYAL AGENTS
OF MI6
Make Me Shiver
Drive Me Wilder
Feel My Pinch
Chase My Shadow
Find My Angel

K19 SECURITY
SOLUTIONS TEAM ONE
Razor's Edge
Gunner's Redemption
Mistletoe's Magic
Mantis' Desire
Dutch's Salvation

K19 SECURITY
SOLUTIONS TEAM TWO
Striker's Choice
Monk's Fire
Halo's Oath
Tackle's Honor
Onyx's Awakening

K19 SHADOW OPERATIONS
TEAM ONE
Code Name: Ranger
Code Name: Diesel
Code Name: Wasp
Code Name: Cowboy
Code Name: Mayhem

K19 ALLIED INTELLIGENCE
TEAM ONE
Code Name: Ares
Code Name: Cayman
Code Name: Poseidon
Code Name: Zeppelin
Code Name: Magnet

K19 ALLIED INTELLIGENCE
TEAM TWO
Coming Soon:
Code Name: Puck
Code Name: Michelangelo
Code Name: Typhon
Code Name: Hornet
Code Name: Reaper

PROTECTORS
UNDERCOVER
Undercover Agent
Undercover Emissary
Coming Soon:
Undercover Savior
Undercover Infidel
Undercover Assassin

THE INVINCIBLES
TEAM ONE
Decked
Edged
Grinded
Riled
Smoked

THE INVINCIBLES
TEAM TWO
Bucked
Irished
Sainted
Hammered
Ripped

THE UNSTOPPABLES
TEAM ONE
Furied
Merried

COWBOYS OF
CRESTED BUTTE
A Cowboy Falls
A Cowboy's Dance
A Cowboy's Kiss
A Cowboy Stays
A Cowboy Wins

Table of Contents

1

Fury

There was nothing like the burn of a neat shot of bourbon as the smooth liquid slid down my throat. I considered it a reminder of how pleasure could follow pain. As the warmth settled in my stomach, then coursed through my veins, I looked over at the man who'd been my friend with benefits, watching as he danced with the new woman in his life.

In all the years I'd known him, Rip never once gazed at me the way he looked at Pearl. It hurt, but it was my pride that was wounded, not my heart. I'd known all along, in the same way he did, that we weren't "the one" for each other.

Rip had found his "it" girl, and I was glad for him in the same way he'd be happy for me if I ever met the man I was meant to spend my life with.

Now, though, sitting at the bar and wishing I was dancing like they were, sucked. Big time. Sure, there were a few men here tonight I could ask to two-step me around the crowded dance floor, and I'd certainly never been accused of being shy, but my heart wasn't in it.

Instead, I signaled Rebel, the bartender closest to me, for another shot.

"How ya doin' tonight, Fury?" she asked as she filled my empty glass with two fingers of the smoky dark-amber liquor I'd grown to love.

"You want the truth or a line?"

She smiled. "Always the truth, my friend."

"I'm feeling like the odd man out, as they say."

"I get that, this bein' a private party and all. No strangers here tonight; just the same ol', same ol'. Not that I care." Rebel was happily married to a man I'd run a few missions with back when I was a CIA operative. I'd left that life, though, to pursue another form of the law as an attorney—what I'd always dreamed of being when I was growing up.

Rebel and her husband, Edge, like Rip and Pearl, were meant to be. Soulmates. Their suns rose and set for each other.

I downed the shot and was about to call it a night when I remembered I got here on my own and was in no shape to drive myself the thirty miles back to my house in the city. Getting a car service here in the hills outside Austin, Texas, would be impossible any night, but more so on Sunday.

"Fuck," I muttered to myself since Rebel had walked away.

"Would you like to dance?" I heard a sultry Spanish-accented voice say from my right at the same time I felt a body brush up against mine. I slowly turned my head to see if the man looked as good as he sounded and was pleasantly surprised to discover he exceeded my hopes.

"Who are you?" I asked, stunned there was anyone here tonight I didn't know, given, as Rebel had said, it was a private party.

"My friends call me Tres."

I looked down the length of him. Good Lord, the man was hotter than a ghost pepper. "How'd you sneak an invite to this shindig, Tres?"

"I'm actually working. I'm head bouncer here at the Long Branch."

"Yeah? Your bosses won't mind if you abandon your duties?"

"They encourage it. Maeve will tell you if you don't dance at least once a night, especially when you're working, you don't belong here."

Maeve, the wife of the attorney whose firm I'd joined a few months ago, was on the dance floor with her husband, Hammer. They'd purchased the bar around the same time the previous owner—Bobby MacIver— retired from "the scene," as he'd told everyone.

I knew the real reason behind his decision, though; Bobby had stage-four cancer and didn't want to spend every night working the kind of hours a place like this required. Maeve and Hammer had been smart to hire a crew capable of running the Branch for them if they needed or wanted time away from it.

A chill coursed through me when Tres trailed his finger from my wrist up to my elbow, and I met his gaze.

"Dance with me, *niña hermosa*."

Between his accent and his classically handsome looks, how could I say no?

When I woke the next morning, my mouth felt as though it had been stuffed with cotton balls. My head throbbed, and I was bare-ass naked—not the way I usually slept. And I wasn't alone. Tres-the-bouncer was in my bed, head propped on his bent arm, staring at me.

Rather than speak, he leaned forward and swirled my nipple with the tip of his tongue. I didn't remember much of last night, but flashbacks of the pleasure his mouth had brought me awakened my every nerve ending.

While I'd normally kick a guy out of my bed long before sunrise, last night, I'd let Tres stay. Maybe the promise of more of the best sex I'd had in my life kept me from giving him the boot. Or maybe I'd been too drunk to care and simply passed out. Not something I was proud of.

Tres kept up his assault on my breasts, alternating between nipples until I began to writhe. Then he spread my legs and cupped my pussy.

"Already so wet for me," he murmured. "I think you like my hands and mouth on your body."

"Shh," I moaned more than said. I didn't want to talk or even listen. I wanted every part of my brain to focus on how what he was doing to me felt.

"I thought you liked the dirty talk," he murmured. "You did last night."

He wasn't wrong. I remembered how each orgasm he'd wrung from me was enhanced by the way he described in great detail how my body made his feel and what he wanted to do to me next.

I shuddered when Tres pushed the bedclothes out of his way and settled himself between my legs. I peeked down to make sure he was wearing a condom, but closed my eyes again as soon as I saw he was.

"I want you to watch. Watch as my *rabo* slides into your *chirri, mi tormenta.*"

The one and only language I spoke was English. However, I didn't need to know a word of Spanish to understand what he wanted me to see.

I cried out when he thrust his massive penis deep inside me. The heat of what I knew would be multiple orgasms spread throughout my body.

Before the last of the shudders of pleasures left me depleted, Tres rolled so I was on top. He grasped both my breasts and pinched my nipples between two fingers. The orgasm I thought had ended kept thundering through me. I arched my back when he put his hands on my waist, holding me in place as he jackhammered into me until I screamed in mind-blowing ecstasy.

"God, you're good at that," I murmured as I rolled off him and onto my back. Chill bumps spread over my skin when he scattered kisses down my side.

"We are not finished, *maravillosa*."

"Yeah, we are." I half laughed, given I didn't have enough energy for a full chuckle, nor did I have enough to ask him what the term of endearment meant.

"I will make you rage again and again, *mi tormenta*."

He'd called me that last night, and when I asked why, he said, "In my country, it is what we call a powerful storm."

Storm was my last name. I'd say it was how I'd gotten my code name—Fury—back when I was still with the CIA, but it wasn't. I'd earned the somewhat disparaging moniker after losing my head in a fit of raging anger. I'd blame it on my youth, except, even though I'd learned to temper my tantrums—in part due to a really good therapist, they still raged beneath the surface when provoked.

My dad was the same way. Except he had my mom to talk him off the ledge when he was about to let his wrath loose. Other than my sister, no other person, let alone a romantic partner, did that for me. Mainly because I never let anyone get close enough to know my struggle with anger management.

When Tres stroked my cheek with his fingertip, I met his gaze. "So lost in thought. What about, I wonder?"

I turned my face away rather than into his touch. "As much as I'd like to lie here in bed with you all day, I have too much to do." I glanced at the clock on the nightstand behind him. "It's already past the time I should've left the house." I was lying. In fact, once he was gone, I'd probably go back to sleep.

Tres grabbed both my wrists, held them over my head with one hand, and kissed me. "Last night, you insisted you had nothing to do today or even for the rest of the week."

"Must've been drunk. In fact, I think we both know I was more than inebriated."

Tres' expression changed. "Don't disparage yourself or us by blaming it on anything other than our bodies being in total sync with one another."

I rolled my eyes. "Yeah, well, some of us have real jobs, which require us to be out of bed before noon every day. So while I may have said something different in the 'heat of the moment,' now I really do have to get to work."

The look on his face was one of amusement. Maybe with a bit of condescension mixed in. As if being a bouncer was far superior to being an attorney. "If your intention was to insult me, you did not."

I laughed. This time heartily, but not sharing the same amusement he appeared to be feeling. "Frankly, I don't care if I insulted you or not." I wrenched my hands from his grasp, got out of bed, and padded over to the bathroom. "It's been fun, Tres. I'm sure you can find your way out." I closed and locked the door behind me.

Maybe it was stupid to leave the guy free to roam around my apartment, but I knew where he worked, and while our jobs were *vastly* different, we did share the same boss.

I took my time, wincing at the places my body hurt after so many months of sexual "inactivity." Until Tres, Rip was the last man I'd had sex with, and it had literally been too long ago for me to remember exactly when that was.

Tres was right about me not having anything to do today or even all week. I didn't have any cases on the docket or clients to meet with since in my new role as attorney of record for the Invincible Intelligence and

Security Group, they were the only client I had. There were things I wanted to do, though.

Maybe I'd get my nails done. Or go by the market. Perhaps get some new clothes. I could wash my car too, since it was covered in dust from being out at the Long Branch—*fuck*. My car was at the Long Branch. Dammit. Why hadn't I remembered that while Tres was still here and could give me a lift to pick it up? It wasn't like I had any friends I could ask. I supposed Hammer was a friend, but he'd be busy with his wife. Rip too. Not that Pearl was his wife yet, but I doubted he'd appreciate an interruption from me, his former lover, asking for a ride to my car since I'd been too drunk to drive it home last night.

I shrugged a shoulder, knowing I'd be forced to hire a car service that would charge me an astronomical fee to drive me out to the boonies. I hated spending so much money—since I was ridiculously tightfisted—but I could certainly afford it. Having grown up poor, I'd vowed never to be again. I saved half of everything I earned, and I was making more money now than I'd ever imagined possible.

When I came out of the bedroom, an aroma that was distinctly coffee overwhelmed my senses. Bless that man if he'd made a pot before he left.

Rather than get dressed before checking, I strolled toward the kitchen in nothing but a towel, shrieking when I bumped into Tres and the cup of coffee he was carrying in the direction of my bedroom ended up crashing to the floor, spraying both of our nearly naked bodies with hot, steamy liquid.

"¡Dios mío!" he shouted, racing back toward the kitchen, presumably to grab paper towels.

I couldn't wait that long. I dropped my bath towel and used it to wipe away the scalding coffee that had landed on my legs and feet.

Instead of paper towels, Tres came back with what appeared to be almost every dish towel I owned.

"Stand on this before you cut your feet," he said, dropping one to the floor. He took the others and, as I picked up the bath towel and laid it in front of me, proceeded to wipe off both my feet, my ankles, and my legs.

"Um, Tres, I got it all," I said once he reached my knees.

"I need to be sure." He pulled the towel from my hands, tossed it behind him, then used his hands and mouth to check my skin for any more splatters.

"None landed there," I moaned when he reached the apex of my thighs and parted my legs. I weaved my fingers in his hair, steadying myself as he licked through my folds. "Tres, God," I moaned again when he spread me open more and sucked on my clit.

I leaned against the wall as another powerful orgasm left me almost unable to stand. When Tres swept me into his arms and carried me to the bedroom, I didn't bother protesting, simply because I didn't want to.

2

Tres

I'd never known a woman whose body was as perfect as Ellison Storm's. She was exquisitely beautiful even with the frown she wore most of the time. And when her full lips went from pouting to smiling, the way her entire face transformed took my breath away.

While she hadn't seen me before last night, I certainly noticed her. When I found her sitting alone at the bar where I was working as a bouncer, I knew I had to ask her to dance.

As I'd told Ellison last night, my boss and her husband encouraged the staff to dance. Perhaps not the night away, but if we didn't enjoy ourselves when we were there, according to them, we had no business working at the Long Branch.

Me? I loved it there. Dancing or not. Compared to the stress of my life before I came to America from Spain, it was like my entire existence was a vacation.

I spent my days working out, honing my body as well as my mind, then at night, I went to a place known for its good food, better liquor, and live music. Every now and then, women looking for a moment of fun came in. None as beautiful as Ellison, though.

Her big hazel eyes met mine as I rested her body on the bed we'd left less than an hour ago. The morning light streaming in through the windows cast a warm glow on her flawless skin.

"Tres?" she said, holding her hand out to me.

I shook my head. "Let me look at you."

Her cheeks flushed, making me smile.

"It is good for you to wait, *maravillosa*."

"What does that word mean?"

"Many things," I said as I slowly trailed my fingers from the hollow of her neck down her body. "Wonderful is one meaning, but for you, it means *mágica*. Open," I said, bringing my fingers back to her mouth. "Get them wet for me."

When she did, I pulled them from between her lips, blew on the tips, then swirled them around her nipples. Her back arched, and I didn't need to feel her *chirri—* pussy—to know how wet she was. I did anyway.

Ellison hissed when I thrust them inside her. "You are sore. I will be gentle," I said, bending over to quiet her pain with my tongue. Once I'd settled between her legs, I took my time, bringing her to the brink of exploding in pleasure, then easing back before it crescendoed.

"You're making me crazy," she cried after the third time I did it.

"It is my intention. I want you crazy with desire, *mi tormenta.*"

"It's working," she whined.

When I did it for the fourth time, I saw the flare of anger in her eyes. It's what I'd been striving for. I wanted her to unleash herself, let go, and give in to the passion that swirled between us. She tried to grab my cock, but I moved out of her reach.

"Give it to me, dammit," she pleaded.

"You will earn it first."

Her eyes bored into mine. "How?"

"You will come by my hand and mouth as many times as I want. Then I will fuck you."

"Please. God. I can't." She was so far on the edge her eyes filled with tears.

"Give me just one more."

"Tres!" She clenched my fingers when she screamed my name. Then, as promised, I fucked her. After, I

held her in my arms as she slept—knowing I had met my match.

"I'm hungry," she groaned when she woke only one hour later.

When I kissed her cheek and pinched her nipple, my cock was immediately rock-hard again. "I will feed you."

"I can't believe I'm saying this, but no more sex, Tres. I need a break."

I smiled. "For now."

When she made it almost all the way to the kitchen earlier, before I spilled hot coffee on both our bodies, I'd taken food from the refrigerator to make her breakfast. I kissed her palm and got out of bed. When I pulled my boxer briefs on, she got up too.

"Go in and run a bath," I said, pointing to the lavatory.

"But I'm starving."

I walked around the end of the bed and cupped her cheek. "And I promised to feed you. Now, do as I say and run the bath."

"You're bossy."

As she walked away, I swatted her lush ass. "And you love it."

Once I heard the water running, I went into the kitchen. I first brewed another pot of coffee, then made vegetable omelets from what I found in her refrigerator. I cut the baguette I'd taken from her walk-in pantry and put butter and raspberry jam into small bowls. After plating everything I'd prepared, I put it on a tray I found in the cabinet and carried it into the lavatory where she soaked in the tub big enough for both of us.

I gently set it on the counter and returned to the kitchen to bring the coffee on another tray along with cream and sugar. When I walked in the second time, her eyes were open.

"I was hoping there was more coffee."

"How do you take it?"

"A little cream and more sugar."

I watched her face, and after I'd put one teaspoonful in, I added a second. When she smiled, I set the spoon down, added the cream, and handed her the cup. I picked up her plate and fork from the tray and sat on the deck surrounding the tub.

"Open," I said, bringing the first forkful to her lips.

"Breakfast in bathtub? This is different."

"It is one of my favorite things."

"Feeding me?" She laughed when I brought another forkful to her mouth.

"*Sí, mi tormenta.*"

Ellison motioned to the other plate. "You should eat yours before it gets cold."

"I will worry about me after I've taken care of you."

Her cheeks flushed again, and her nipples hardened. When I brought a piece of the bread slathered with butter and jam to her lips, she licked them.

"Are you sure about that?" she asked, eyeing my erection as it strained against my briefs.

"Always."

"Get in," she said, sliding forward after she'd finished the food from her plate.

I removed my underwear and climbed in behind her. When she got to her feet, I grabbed her wrist.

"It's my turn to feed you." She got out, eyeing my coffee. "You take it black."

I nodded as my gaze lingered on her wet, naked body. She handed me the cup, then returned with the plate, just like I'd done with her.

I let her feed me a few bites, shifted to my knees, and stuck my finger in the bowl of jam. I covered both her nipples with it before licking off the sticky sweetness.

"You need to eat," Ellison said, trying to pull away from me.

I snaked my arm around her waist. "I am eating."

"How did my car get here?" Ellison asked an hour later when we carried our dishes to the kitchen and she peeked out the window.

"Rojo drove it here, and Bunker gave him a ride home."

She spun around. "How did he get my keys?"

"You handed them to me before we left, saying I shouldn't let you drive."

"Oh." Her cheeks flamed. "I want you to know I don't drink that much very often."

"I know." I filled the sink with soapy water, plunged the dishes in, and washed them.

"I can do that," she said. "You probably need to get going."

"I know," I repeated. "And no, I don't need to go anywhere."

"You aren't, you know...I mean, you do have a place to go, right?"

I laughed out loud. "Yes, *mi tormenta*. You needn't worry. I have a home. If I am here, it is because I want to be."

"Sorry, I just, I mean…Never mind."

When she finished drying the dishes I'd washed, I took the towel from her hands and tossed it on the counter. "I want to spend the day with you."

"Tres…I…God, what is wrong with me? I can't seem to string an entire sentence together. Look, I don't do the boyfriend thing, okay? We had fun. A lot of fun, in fact, but now, it's over. You go back to your life, and I'll stay here in mine."

While the beautiful Ellison remembered our lovemaking throughout the night, she obviously did not recall that, shortly after we arrived here, she'd poured her heart out to me while we sat, her between my legs, resting against my chest. As I spoon-fed her lime sorbetto, she'd confessed to me how lonely she felt.

"Do you know what I have to do tomorrow?"

"I do not," I'd answered.

"Nothing. In fact, I could go several days without seeing a single other person. How pathetic is it that in order to have someone to talk to, I have to go to the market? I tried making friends at the gym, but I either got dirty looks from the other women, or the men thought I was hitting on them." She'd turned her body toward mine and wrapped her arms around me. "When do you have to be at work?"

"Not for three more days."

"Will you stay, Tres?"

I'd brought my lips to hers and told her my kiss was the promise I would.

"What are you thinking about?"

I looked into her eyes. "A promise I made."

After Ellison poured more coffee, she sat on the sofa. "To whom?"

I got another cup and sat beside her. "To you."

"Oh my God." She rested her head against the cushion, closed her eyes, and groaned.

I leaned over and kissed her cheek. "I promised I would not leave, and I do not break a vow once made."

"Even if I blame it on my being really drunk? I know I keep saying that…"

"How about this? We forget about the conversation you don't remember much of anyway and just enjoy the day. What do you like to do? You mentioned the gym and the market."

"I'm not sure I'm up for a workout, and we just ate."

"I have an idea."

She opened one eye and glanced at me. "What?"

"I will take you to my favorite outdoor market in all of Austin."

"Where is it?"

"You will see."

"I don't like surprises, Tres."

I picked up her hand and kissed her palm. "You will grow to love them."

3

Fury

As soon as he said "promise," bits and pieces of a conversation we'd had the night before came back to me. I didn't remember much about it, other than I'd made a complete fool of myself by confessing I basically had no life.

"We will stop by my place on the way, so I can change my clothes," he said, following me into the bedroom.

"You don't have to do this. I'm not as pathetic as I sounded."

He snaked an arm around my waist and kissed my neck, right below my ear. "Wear something sexy, *mi tormenta*."

"To an outdoor market in January?"

"You needn't worry," he said, kissing then nibbling my shoulder. "I will make sure you stay warm."

I went into the walk-in closet and grabbed a pair of jeans and a sweatshirt. When I came out, Tres was rummaging through my lingerie drawer. He held up a matching bra and panty set made of red lace and little else. "Wear this," he said, stalking over to me. He took the sweatshirt out of my hands and carried it into the closet.

"Hey, what are you doing?"

"Finding something for you to wear."

I followed him and grabbed the sweatshirt. "I have something to wear. And, by the way, these are not comfortable to wear all day." I dangled the red panties.

"It's fine. I prefer you to not wear any." Tres opened the doors of the wardrobe where I kept my sweaters and pulled out a black turtleneck. I had to admit it was one of my favorites. "Put this on and the jeans. No panties."

I opened my mouth to protest, but his heated gaze made me think better of it. Was it so bad that this *muy caliente* man wanted to see me in something sexy? It wasn't as if he'd picked out one of my barely there dresses. Jeans, a turtleneck, and a sexy bra. As far as going sans underwear, I wasn't opposed to it.

"Do I get to pick out what you wear?" I asked as I stepped into the shower he'd turned on. He walked in and shut the glass door.

"Let me do it," he said when I picked up the bottle of shampoo.

"I can wash my own hair, Tres."

"Not like this," he said. "Turn around and put your hands on the wall."

"You're washing my hair, right?"

"Close your eyes," he whispered.

"Oh my God," I groaned when he wove his fingers into my tresses and massaged my scalp. This was no regular shampoo-basin hair wash from the beauty salon. This was closer to what one might experience at a high-end spa. "You are really good at that," I said as his fingers systematically applied pressure to various parts of my scalp.

"You will discover there are many things I'm good at, *mi tormenta.*"

If it was more like this, I was all in. This was the best sex I'd had in my life, the man cooked and fed me breakfast, and he'd had my car brought here. Plus, he wanted to spend the day with me. It didn't feel forced, either. It felt genuine. Maybe instead of digging my heels into the control-freakish place where my comfort lay, I should relax and let myself "go along for the ride" for once.

Rip, the man who, until last night, had been my latest lover, said something to that effect once. Well, he'd shouted more than said it "You don't have to fucking be in control of everything, Fury. *Jesus.* Go along for the ride every once in a while."

So, what the hell? Today, I'd let go. Tomorrow, I'd take a firm grasp of the reins that kept me comfortably grounded.

I'd heard of the "market" Tres took me to, but I never would've ventured there on my own. Mainly because I couldn't understand a single word anyone spoke. Even when one I knew popped up in a sentence, it was so far out of context, I didn't understand it either.

If I had to describe it to someone, I would say it was a flea market crossed with a farmer's market crossed with an outdoor music festival. A place where you could buy everything from parakeets, pigeons, and chickens to handwoven leather belts, flamboyant dresses being sewn on-site, and the pointiest cowboy boots—made of lizard—I'd ever seen. And the food? Better than I'd had anywhere ever, and when I was in the CIA, I'd traveled to many spectacular places.

After sharing an ear of dressed street corn, Tres told me to take a seat and listen to the music while he brought our next dish.

"What is that?" I asked, breathing in the aroma.

"Chiles en nogada," he answered.

"Which is?"

Tres shook his head. "Taste first."

He cut into the chile and brought the fork to my mouth. I shook my head. "Tell me what's in it."

"Trust me, *mi tormenta.*"

My eyes bored into his, and finally, I nodded and opened my mouth. I closed my eyes and savored too many flavors for me to identify them all.

"More, please," I said after I'd swallowed.

Tres smiled and cut another piece.

"Okay, seriously, tell me what's in it," I said after I'd finished.

"First, a poblano chile is fire-roasted. Then it's stuffed with pork and beef mixed with apples, pears, and *acitrón*, which is like candy and made from cactus. The sauce is made from walnuts and sprinkled with parsley and pomegranate seeds."

I reached over and cut another piece myself. "Can we get more?"

Tres smiled. "Not today."

I pouted. "Why not?"

He leaned forward so his mouth was near my ear. "There are many new and wonderful things I plan to introduce to you today." He pulled back and stared into my eyes like he had a few minutes ago. "Will you trust me enough to try?"

I studied him. Could I? Did he have any idea how hard it was for me to do? His eyes never wavered as he waited for the response I finally gave him. "I will."

He leaned closer and kissed me. "Come dance with me."

It was shortly after noon, and there were as many people here as I'd seen the one and only time I attempted to go to SXSW—South by Southwest—before leaving fifteen minutes after I'd arrived, on the verge of a panic attack.

The way Tres held me close and moved us around the dance floor, similarly to how he made love, made the crowds fade away. Like everything else I'd seen and experienced with him thus far, he was fabulous at it.

We danced the afternoon away, taking breaks to sample more food.

"Are you from Mexico?" I asked when he brought a plate of churros topped with fried ice cream.

He shook his head. "My family is from Spain."

Before I could ask more, he brought a fork to my lips, and I opened them to take a bite. At first, I felt uncomfortable with him feeding me. Now, though, it just seemed sexy as fuck. In fact, I hoped our eating dessert meant he would be ready to head back to my place.

"What are you thinking about, Ellison?" he asked, grinning.

"Why do you ask?" I teased.

"Your cheeks"—he reached up and stroked one—"are flushed and your pupils are dilated."

"Maybe it's the churro."

Tres slowly shook his head. "I think it's something else."

"I guess you'll have to wait and take me home to find out."

Except he didn't wait. When we arrived at his vehicle, he pushed me up against the door, reached down the front of my jeans, and cupped my drenched pussy. "Not the churro," he said as he stroked through my folds with his fingers. I clung to him when my knees gave out.

"Tres," I moaned.

"Shh, *mi tormenta.* You don't want anyone to hear and walk over to see what I am doing to you."

I could barely make out his words over the roar of blood coursing through my veins. When he pressed the pad of a second finger on my clit, I had to bite my tongue to keep from crying out. Tres held me until I slowly recovered from the powerful orgasm that racked my body. When he pulled his hand out and licked his finger, I felt a second one coming on. Or maybe it was just a continuation of the first.

We were barely through the door of my house before we were tearing at each other's clothes. After pulling my sweater over my head, Tres grabbed my wrists when I reached behind to unfasten my bra.

"Leave it," he demanded before kneeling in front of me and unfastening my jeans. He slid them down, over my ass, to my ankles. "Step out."

"Wait."

Tres looked up at me. "What is it?"

"Stand up."

He did as I asked, brow furrowed, eyes questioning.

"It's my turn." I stood in front of him as he had me, pulling his shirt over his head, then knelt as I unfastened his belt, then his jeans.

"Mi tormenta," he groaned when I pushed him back against the wall and took him into my mouth. I couldn't help but smile as I thought about the number of times in the last several hours that he had *tormented* me, forcing me to succumb to endless waves of pleasure derived from his hands, tongue, and cock. I had every intention of doing the same to him with my fingers, lips, and body.

Rather than ravishing each other throughout the night, Tres and I slept soundly. We were both exhausted from having had little sleep the night before, combined with eating, drinking, and dancing all afternoon and into the evening.

When I woke, he wasn't in bed beside me, but I could hear him out in the kitchen. As I rolled over and saw it was a little past seven, I thought about going back to sleep, although I doubted I'd be able to. Any minute now, Tres would return, probably bringing me a cup of coffee to ease the blow of him saying it had been fun, but it was time for him to leave.

This was the exact reason I never let a man spend the night. I wanted to be the one to send him packing, not be the one left behind. I'd been "left behind" once in my life, and it hadn't been after a one-night stand. No, that time, it was my entire future I'd been left to figure out by myself.

I'd broken every one of my rules with Tres. I'd let him stay not one but *two* nights. Making matters worse, I'd let alcohol lower my defenses and had actually confessed to him that I was lonely.

I shuddered and hugged myself, realizing I already wished he would stay. Every minute we'd spent together had been easy—and wonderful. Tres was fun, in bed and out. Our conversations flowed so naturally I felt as though I'd known him for several months. He made me laugh, brought me out of my shell, introduced me to new things, and kissed me like I never had been. The way he looked at me, too, seemed so much like how I'd seen Hammer look at Maeve and Rip look at Pearl.

I shook my head. Now, I was just being stupid. I could still recover this, though. So I got out of bed, raced into the closet, and put on a pair of joggers, then pulled a sports bra and T-shirt over my head and grabbed my socks and running shoes. I'd just finished tying the laces when Tres returned to the bedroom, carrying two steaming mugs.

"Thanks," I said, taking the cup, but setting it on the dresser.

"Where are we off to this morning?" he asked, leaning against the doorjamb.

"To meet a friend I run with a couple of times a week." It wasn't exactly true. I did know someone who ran along the river almost every day, and sometimes, I showed up and ran with him. He wasn't really a "friend" either. More someone I worked with. I looked over at the place on the dresser where I usually kept my key fob but didn't see it. "Do you, uh, happen to know where my car key is?"

Tres nodded.

"Where?"

He curled his finger, motioning me toward him. Instead, I looked at my watch. "Sorry. If I don't leave now, I'm going to be late." I walked out of the room, hoping I'd find the fob on the kitchen counter. I didn't.

"Tres?" I called out, not wanting to retrace my steps and wind up back in the bedroom with him. "Where is it?"

I heard his footsteps headed in my direction and rolled my shoulders. I could still do this. Even if it meant leaving with him still here. When he joined me in the kitchen, he had my cup of coffee along with his. He set them on the counter, reached into his pocket, and pulled out the fob.

"Thanks," I said, snapping it up. I leaned forward and kissed his cheek. "I had a great time. Thank you. But I really gotta run, so, uh, maybe you could grab your stuff?"

"I will run with you."

"Tres, seriously, I—"

He cut me off with one of his toe-curling kisses. He gripped my neck so, when his lips released mine, I couldn't back away. "I will run with you," he repeated.

"You don't have to."

He smiled and kissed the tip of my nose. "I told you I promised I wouldn't leave. And no matter how hard you push me away, I will not let you."

I stared into his eyes. "Why not?" I whispered.

"You know why, *mi tormenta*. You feel it as much as I do."

"Feel what?" I said, still whispering.

He put my hand on his heart. "You and I are connected. *Mágica.*"

While my first inclination would normally be to roll my eyes and laugh, this time, I didn't. I could feel the sincerity of his words as much as the connection he spoke of. Was it crazy? Probably. Could I resist him, knowing deep in my heart that, as much as my brain tried to deny it, I loved spending time with this man?

"You agree?"

I slowly nodded.

Tres pulled me closer to him, let out a deep breath, and looked up at the ceiling, almost as if he was saying a silent prayer. "Wait here," he said, pointing to the floor.

This time, I did laugh. "Right here? Right in this very spot? I can't move even a little?"

"If you do as I say, I'll make it worth your while later."

"Promise?" I winked.

Tres gripped the back of my neck and kissed me as if that sealed yet another vow between us.

4

Tres

I cupped the cheek of the only woman I wished I could tell the truth. Whom I wished I had told the truth the first night I spent with her. The same night I promised to stay. In a few days, though, I'd have to leave. I couldn't remain with her longer than that.

While I didn't know the specifics of what had happened that made Ellison afraid to trust, afraid to let someone in, afraid to love, I knew what I was about to do would result in her heart breaking all over again.

Did I have a choice? I suppose I could return home, try to make things right with my family, try to get them—no, not them, him—to understand I couldn't live his life. Even to do that, I'd have to leave without Ellison knowing where I'd gone. I could only hope that when I returned, she'd forgive me, give me another chance. Until then, I planned to spend every minute I could with her. Make sure she felt the connection between us as strongly as I did.

"Ready?" I asked when I returned to the kitchen and found her in the exact spot I'd told her to wait. I'd promised if she did, I'd make it worth it. If she didn't seem so determined to go for a run, I'd show her my appreciation now. I'd make love to her body in the way we both knew only I could do. No other man had ever made her feel as good as I did. It wasn't just my ego talking. I knew it in my heart. Our bodies were a perfect fit, a perfect match.

"Tres, if there are other things you need to do, it's okay. I won't be—"

I kissed her. Every time she tried to push me away, that's what I planned to do. Kiss her to remind her I was staying—for as long as I could.

"I guess that's a no," Ellison said with a laugh I'd learned hid her insecurities.

"We're spending the day together, *mi tormenta*. Just like we did yesterday."

By the time we got to the park on the edge of the Colorado River, the area was deserted. Ellison said her friend must've already left on his run. Her disappointment in missing him made me feel the type of jealousy I rarely had. My Hispanic blood ran hot in all things, but when it came to love, it boiled. No one could dispute Ellison was mine. She had been since the first moment I held her in my arms.

"What are you thinking about?" she asked as we stretched before hitting the trail.

"I confess to being happy not to have to share you this day."

She smiled, and her cheeks flushed. "Tres…"

I waited for her to protest, but she did not. If she had, it would have been akin to a lie. She loved the attention I showered on her. She basked in its glow like a cat reveling in the heat of a warm ray of sunshine.

Her brow furrowed when her mobile rang, and she checked the screen.

"Is everything okay?" I asked.

"Um, yeah," she said without looking up at me. "It's my sister."

"You should answer," I suggested when she bit her bottom lip.

"It's okay. I'll call her back."

When the phone stopped ringing, I walked over and put my arm around her waist. "Would you like privacy to speak with her?"

"It's okay," she repeated.

I took her hand and led her toward the parking lot.

"Wait," she gasped. "What about our run?"

"You will call your sister, and while you do, I'll walk over and get us both some water." I pointed to a coffee stand. "When you are finished, join me, and we'll continue our day."

"I talk to my sister almost every day, so if I don't answer—"

I leaned down and kissed her. "You do not need to justify talking to your family, *mi tormenta*."

5

Fury

"Is everything okay, Stephanie?" I asked when my sister answered.

"I called to ask you the same thing. I figured you were busy yesterday, but when you didn't check in this morning, I decided I should, instead."

"I'm sorry. Like you said, I've been, um, busy."

"I see," my sister said with a lilt in her voice, suggesting she knew exactly what had been occupying my time. "What's his name?"

"Tres," I whispered even though I was in the car, the doors and windows were closed, and I could see him walking over to the coffee stand, which was several feet away.

"Yeah? Tell me about him."

"He's…overwhelming."

"I see," she repeated. "Making you step out of your comfort zone?"

"More like pulling me kicking and screaming."

"It's time someone did. How many years has it been, Ell?"

I could pretend I didn't know what she meant, but we both knew I did. "Too many to even bring it up. That has nothing to do with—"

"The reason you push every decent guy you meet away? Is that what you were going to say? Because that's the truth."

"Stephanie, I am an attorney, and before that, I was—"

"I know, I know. You were a CIA agent. Yes, I've heard it all before. I also know your idea of a long-term relationship is letting your 'dates' stay past three in the morning before kicking them to the curb. So, tell me more about Tres. How'd you meet? What does he do? What's he like?"

"He's…nice. I met him at a private party some friends threw last weekend." I lowered my voice again, as if someone could hear me. "He's a bouncer."

"Ah, a bouncer."

"What does that mean?" I asked.

"You tell me."

"It just means…"

"What? That he's the greatest guy who's ever lived? Because I can tell you Jimmy is, and that's what he was doing when I met him."

"While putting himself through graduate school."

"Are you saying that if he hadn't been, he wouldn't have been good enough for me?"

"*Stephanie!* I didn't say that at all."

"But for some reason, you felt compelled to *whisper* when you told me what he did for a living." My sister sighed. "Look, I know you worked hard to get where you are in life. I know how important success is to you. But, Ell, success isn't all about work. I didn't go to college, and maybe I'm not what most would consider 'successful,' but I'm *happy*. I'm with a man I adore and who loves me as much as I love him. We have two amazing kids, and I get to stay at home with them, volunteer at their school, and be team mom for the sports they play. Having time to spend with them and Jimmy is what's important to me."

"Then, I would think you'd understand my career is important to me."

"I do understand that, but, Ellison, can you honestly say you're happy?"

"This conversation is pointless. Are we still on for dinner this week?"

"Of course we are. And if you want to bring Tres, he'd be welcome too."

I laughed. "I think you might be jumping the gun just a little."

"Ell, every guy you meet isn't Blake. Not every guy lies and cheats. Not every guy is going to break your heart if you crack it open enough to let them in. It's been over ten years since you've been in a relationship, Ellison. Let it go and get on with your life. You never know when the man you are really meant to be with is going to knock on your door. Let him in when he does, sis."

"Listen, I gotta go, but I'll see you on Wednesday."

"At least consider bringing Tres with you. I'd like to meet him."

"I'll let you know." I looked up, and even from this distance, Tres' eyes bored into mine.

There was more to him than what was immediately apparent. He obviously took great care of himself, but it went beyond that. The man was impeccably dressed, even when only wearing jeans and a shirt. He carried himself like someone who was comfortable in his own skin, self-assured, and was as well-spoken as he was well-groomed. Was it so hard to imagine a man who earned a living as a bouncer could be all those things?

And the way he looked at me—I couldn't remember the last time I felt as though someone truly *saw* me. My sister knew me better than anyone, even our mom. As hard as it was to hear some of what she'd said, it was only because it was true.

Blake, the guy she mentioned, had been the love of my life. Or so I'd thought until I arrived at his college dorm as a surprise and, instead, found him in bed with a woman I learned he'd been in a relationship with since the beginning of the previous semester. The same woman he'd eventually married and had two kids with. Everything I'd heard about Blake hurt. Discovering they'd named their kids Liam and Olivia—the names he and I had picked for the children we'd planned to have one day—shattered what little was left of my heart.

Blake was the reason I'd abandoned my dream of becoming an attorney and, instead, went after a job with the CIA. I remembered one of the first questions I'd asked in my initial interview was how much international travel would be involved. When the agent conducting the interview told me I could essentially travel as much as I wanted to, I knew I'd do anything to get hired. All I'd wanted was to get as far away from Blake Howell as I possibly could.

Serendipitously, years later, I'd been on a mission with Keon "Edge" Edgemon and Miles "Grinder" Stone when I met Sterling Anderson, aka Hammer. At the time, he'd been the attorney of record for the private intelligence firm Edge and Grinder founded along with Decker Ashford and Cortez "Rile" DeLéon.

One night, over dinner with the team, I'd admitted to Hammer I once aspired to be an attorney. Evidently, through our conversations, he saw something in me I'd believed long since buried, and he encouraged me not to let my childhood dream die. With him as a mentor, I left the agency, returned to college, and eventually passed the bar. A few months after I had, he asked me to join his firm as the sole other partner. I'd taken over as attorney of record for the Invincibles, and Hammer was all but retired, happy to be running the Long Branch, where I'd met Tres, and spending as much time as he could with his wife, the love of his life. They had one baby girl, named for her mother, and while neither had said anything, I didn't doubt another child would be on his or her way soon.

While my thoughts wandered, Tres' gaze remained on mine. Since I no longer held the phone to my ear, his expression shifted to puzzled. I got out of the car and walked in his direction. Rather than approach me, he remained seated.

"My sister was worried after I didn't return an earlier call," I explained when I got close enough for him to hear me.

Tres reached his hand out to me, and I took it. "What did you tell her?"

"That I've been busy."

He raised a brow.

"She asked your name."

"And?"

"She told me to invite you to dinner on Wednesday."

Tres' brow furrowed, and I pulled my hand away.

"You don't have to come, of course. I just—"

He stood and kissed me.

"You do that to shut me up, don't you?" I asked, pulling away.

Tres ran his finger over my lower lip. "I do it because I can't resist."

I rolled my eyes and attempted to step back, but Tres snaked his arm around my waist, holding me close enough that I could feel his desire for me.

"What did you say when she told you to invite me to join you?"

I didn't want to confess how I'd responded, but I couldn't lie. "I suggested she was jumping the gun."

He nodded slowly.

"Tres, I…" I'd hoped he'd silence me with another kiss, but he didn't. "Would you like to come?"

"I would."

My eyes darted back and forth between his. "Why?"

"You already know the answer."

"Just because I confessed my loneliness in a weak and somewhat inebriated moment, it doesn't mean you're bound to me for all eternity." My intention was to make a joke, but it didn't come out that way.

"And if I want to be bound to you until the end of time, what would you say to that?" he asked.

"I'd say you were crazy," I whispered. I'd expected to see hurt in his eyes. Instead, I saw mirth.

"Mi tormenta," he sighed, shaking his head. "You are right. I am crazy for you."

I smiled. "I'm crazy for you too." I stunned myself with the admission, but I couldn't deny the truth of it.

"Your honesty humbles me."

"Tres?"

He smiled like I had. "Yes?"

"Never mind." As much as I wanted to know more about him, something told me to wait. That I might discover something I wished I hadn't.

"If you change your mind, let me know," he responded, almost as if he could read my thoughts.

"We should run."

His look of amusement was back. "Are you certain you want to?" he asked after I'd done nothing to hide my hesitation.

"No, but I'll be glad I did once we're finished."

Tres' expression changed.

"Running, I mean."

He pulled me closer, if that were possible, and rested his head against mine. "I knew what you meant, sweet Ellison."

As we took off down the trail, a feeling of dread, or maybe foreboding, settled in my chest. No matter how hard I pounded the dirt beneath my feet, it didn't get better; it worsened.

We'd gone a little over two miles when we ran past the city docks. I stopped when I realized Tres had. I backtracked and looked over his shoulder at the piece of paper he was holding. He turned his head and kissed me. "Up for a paddle?" he asked.

"Kayaking is one of my favorite things to do."

"Mine as well. You won't mind cutting our run short?"

"Not at all," I said, laughing at how out of breath I was. "You aren't just showing pity on me, are you?" I asked, noting he wasn't even breathing heavily.

He smiled, kissed me again, and walked down to the dock.

Within minutes, we were out on the Colorado River, him in the back and me in the front of a double kayak. It was something I'd never thought I'd do, always scoffing at the couples I'd see out on the water. I'd shake my head, inwardly chastising the woman for being "lazy" while her beau paddled her across the calm river. Now,

I had to admit my disparaging thoughts were really just me envying the relationship I knew I'd probably never have. Here I was, though, happily sitting back and resting the oar across my lap when Tres told me to relax and enjoy the ride.

We went as far as the second city dock, where Tres paddled us to the shore after asking if I was as hungry as he was. Phrased that way, I had no trouble admitting I was famished.

We walked a few blocks to Penny's, a sidewalk café known for its wide variety of eggs Benedict. I could never eat an entire serving, so I was all for it when Tres suggested we share.

"What's your favorite?" he asked.

"You pick."

He studied the menu for a few seconds, then raised his head. "You like the crab and crawfish best."

"Good guess," I responded, chuckling.

Tres shook his head. "I wasn't guessing."

"Either way, yes, that's my favorite."

After he'd ordered, asking for two plates, he reached over and took my hand. "I like being with you, Ellison."

"I like being with you too," I said, knowing my cheeks had flushed.

"It is hard for you to admit."

I nodded. "It is."

He brought my hand to his lips and kissed the back of it. "Who made you afraid to love?"

I tried to pull away, but he held tight.

"Tell me," he whispered, kissing my palm.

I turned my head. "No one."

"Lying does not become you, *maravillosa*."

My eyes filled with tears I knew were impossible to stop from falling. "He didn't make me afraid to love. He made me stop believing in it." Again, the ease of the admission stunned me.

"I hate him."

His comment made me laugh. "I do too."

Tres moved to the seat beside me and put his arm across the back of my chair. "It is real, Ellison," he said. "Don't doubt it."

"It's hard, Tres."

"Trust what you feel."

I smiled. "Trusting what I feel is what's led me to stop believing in it."

"I will change your mind."

"Will you?" I said, barely above a whisper.

"I promise."

I wanted to believe him. I *longed* to believe him. But could I? Blake's betrayal had devastated me. Because of him, I'd vowed never to let anyone close enough to hurt me again. Other than my sister and our parents, I'd managed to keep everyone else at arm's length. Even Hammer, who I considered a friend, didn't *really* know me. I wiped at my tears, hating my self-pity.

"Can we change the subject?"

Rather than answer, Tres leaned forward and kissed me. I'd never been fond of PDA, but like the kayak ride, I'd admit my distaste was based mainly on envy.

"When do you have to be at the Long Branch again?" I asked once we paddled to where we'd originally rented the kayak and were walking to the parking lot.

"Not until Thursday," Tres said, squeezing my hand. "Which means I'd very much like to join you for dinner with your family."

"You don't have to—"

I didn't complain or pull away when Tres shut me up again with a kiss.

After we returned the kayaks, Tres and I spent a couple of hours at Austin's Museum of the Weird followed by a late-afternoon picnic at the Umlauf Sculpture Garden. Neither of which I'd heard of, let alone visited.

We were about to head home when we saw a sign for the Haunted ATX Tour. Tres called the number, and a few minutes later, we were met by a hearse that had been converted into a limo. Once we'd paid for our tickets, two very goth-looking women drove us around downtown Austin, pointing out all the places believed to be haunted. I doubted our tour guides appreciated our laughing through most of it.

Once back at my house, Tres stopped me before I was able to enter the code on the keypad that would unlock my door.

"What?" I asked.

"Take off your clothes."

I laughed and reached up to attempt to enter the code a second time. He grabbed my wrist and pulled my arm away.

"Strip for me, *mi tormenta*," he said as he reached down the front of my shorts and cupped my pussy. "You cannot lie and say you don't want to; you are dripping with desire to do as I say."

"Let me go inside first," I whined, resting my back against his front when he thrust two fingers into me as his thumb circled my clit.

"Can you feel how much it excites me to have you do as I tell you?"

"I haven't done it yet."

"But you will," he murmured, nibbling on my neck as he pressed his fingers against my G-spot. I was on the verge of an orgasm when he pulled them from inside me, removed his hand from the front of my pants, and took a step back. "Remove your clothes now, Ellison."

I reached for him, but he took another step away. "Do it for me," I pleaded.

He smiled and shook his head. "I want to see you with nothing on your body but moonlight."

"Someone will see."

He breathed in deeply before taking yet another step in the opposite direction of where I wanted him to be. "The idea they will excites you even more."

I grasped the hem of my shirt.

"Shorts first."

When I toed off my shoes and lowered my pants along with my panties, Tres cupped his erection through his shorts as he stalked toward me. He knelt on the cement step, put his hand behind my right knee, and lifted it over his shoulder. He wrapped one arm around me. "Remove your shirt and bra."

"Tres—"

"Do as I say, Ellison."

I stared into Tres' eyes, steadied myself with one hand on his shoulder, and attempted to remove my shirt with the other.

"Now, your bra," he said when I finally managed to get it over my head. "Play with your nipples," he said when I dropped my bra where my shirt had fallen. "Both hands. I will not let you fall."

I followed his orders as he used his hands and mouth to torment me, driving me over the edge into ecstasy again and again while I stood right outside the back door of my house with nothing more than him and the moonlight on my skin.

6

Fury

By Wednesday afternoon, I'd given up suggesting Tres leave, or bothering to fabricate something requiring me to go to the office, or trying to push him away. I really liked spending time with him—both in and out of bed. Although the former continued to be off-the-charts fantastic.

"There's still time to back out," I said as we lingered in the bathtub before going to my sister's house for dinner.

Tres responded the same way he often did, by kissing me. This time, from just under my ear, down my neck, to my shoulder. At the same time, he reached around and pinched my nipples with one hand while he did the same with my clit, using his other.

"No!" I cried when he suddenly stopped and stood, pulling me out of the water with him.

"We must leave soon," he said as he used the towel to dry me off before doing the same to himself.

"You are not seriously suggesting we leave now?"

Tres captured one of my nipples between two fingers. "Your sister will not think highly of me if we arrive late."

Late? I didn't want to go at all, given my current level of sexual frustration.

"Hi, I'm Stephanie Sanders, and this is my husband, Jimmy," my sister said when they both came to the front door before I had the chance to open it. "Hey, sis," she added when I attempted to look around her.

"Who else is here?" I asked, hearing voices coming from inside.

"Haley and JJ—"

"There she is," I heard my father say before my sister could finish her sentence.

I grabbed her arm. "Are you fucking kidding me?" I whispered in her ear. "Mom and Dad are here, and you didn't tell me?"

"They just got here."

"Hey, Ell. Come give your ol' dad a hug hello."

"You are in so much trouble," I said to my sister as I squeezed around her to greet our parents. "Stephanie didn't tell me you guys were in town," I said, hugging and kissing my mom after my dad.

My mom looked puzzled. "She didn't? She knew we were coming."

"She probably wanted it to be a surprise," said my dad, looking in the direction of the door, where I'd left Tres to fend for himself. "Who's that?" he asked.

I walked back over to where Jimmy was escorting him inside. "Tres, I'd like you to meet my father, Jason, and my mom, Janice."

He stepped forward and shook my dad's hand. "Leandro Barello, but everyone calls me Tres." He turned to my mom and took her hand, but rather than shake it, he kissed the back of it.

Her eyes met mine, and she wiggled her eyebrows. "How long have the two of you been seeing each other?"

"We're just friends," I said.

At the same time, Tres said, "A few days."

My father raised a brow and turned to me. "A few days?"

"We're friends," I repeated. I doubted either of my parents believed me when Tres put his arm around my shoulders and kissed my cheek.

"What can I get you to drink?" Jimmy asked Tres. "Glass of wine? Beer?"

"I'll have whatever is easiest, thank you," Tres responded.

"Ell? Red or white?" my brother-in-law asked me, knowing I preferred wine over the craft beer he usually had fully stocked.

"White, please."

My sister grabbed my arm and pulled me toward the hallway. "Oh my God," she mouthed. "He's *gorgeous*."

"Your sister's right," said my mom, fanning her face. "And so romantic."

My eyes scrunched. "Romantic?"

She nodded. "Did you see the way he kissed the back of my hand?"

I shifted and turned partway around so I could see into the kitchen, where Tres was still talking with my dad and Jimmy, then looked between my mom and sister. "So, when did you really arrive?"

"I told you they got here a couple of hours ago."

"Did you drive?"

My mom chuckled. "Don't be ridiculous. All the way from North Carolina? No, your sister picked us up at the airport a little after noon."

"Auntie Ell?" I heard my niece say as she came barreling in my direction. She wrapped her arms around my waist like it had been far longer than a week since she last saw me.

"Tell your aunt what you did yesterday," my sister said, folding her arms.

"Uh-oh, puss, what did you do?"

My nephew, three years younger than his sister, came out of his bedroom. "This," he said, pointing to his forehead, where his bangs that had been long enough to touch his eyebrows were now less than a quarter inch in some places.

"You're the one who said he needed a haircut," Haley said to her mother without removing her arms from around my waist.

"While that may be true, I didn't say I wanted *you* to do it."

"I don't think it looks that bad." Haley looked up at me. "Do you?"

I knelt down so I was on her level. "It's pretty bad, puss. How much trouble are you in?"

"She's grounded," Stephanie answered before her daughter could.

"How long?" I asked, again directing the question to my niece.

"Until she says."

"I see." I looked up at Stephanie. "Indefinitely?"

"Or until her brother decides he's no longer too mortified to come out of his room."

Haley gestured at JJ. "He's out of his room right now."

"I'm not all the way out." He pointed to the foot still on the threshold.

"Here you go," said Jimmy, approaching with a glass of wine. "I really like him," he said, motioning with his head in Tres' direction.

"Yeah? You know that after what? Two minutes of conversation?"

"Always trust your first impression," Jimmy said, squeezing past me to pick up his son. "Come on out and meet Auntie Ell's new friend."

I was about to intervene, but when JJ didn't protest, I kept my mouth shut.

"You're still grounded," Stephanie said to Haley as she followed her husband and son into the kitchen.

"He really is dreamy," my mom said as we followed too.

I glanced over my shoulder at her. *"Dreamy?* You sound like Grandma Betty."

She shrugged. "Well, he is."

Maybe the third glass of wine my brother-in-law poured for me partway through dinner had lowered my inhibitions, but when Tres either kept his hand on my leg or rested his arm across the back of my chair, or leaned over and kissed my cheek and told me how much fun he was having, I didn't mind. In fact, I liked it. Especially since he'd won over not just my brother-in-law but my sister, parents, niece, and nephew.

"Ell, is that your phone?" my sister asked when she got up to plate dessert.

"It is. Sorry." I cringed, recognizing it was my work cell ringing rather than my personal phone. I got up and walked over to where I'd set my purse in the living room and pulled it out. When I saw Hammer's name on the screen, I excused myself and stepped outside.

"What's up?" I asked.

"Hey, Fury. Vex has been trying to reach you."

"He has?" I held the phone away from my ear and checked for recent calls. There weren't any. "Maybe he called my other number."

"Either way, he needs your help with something."

"Roger that. I'll reach out," I said, wishing I hadn't had a second glass of wine, let alone a third.

Bronson Dunning, aka Vex, was the man tapped to head up the still-unnamed new unit of the Invincibles. If Hammer said he needed *my* help, that meant legally.

Rather than going back inside to check my other phone, I called him from this one.

"Hello?" he answered.

"Vex, it's Fury. Hammer said you were trying to reach me."

"Yeah, sorry to bother you so late, but I need your help."

I held the phone away a second time and glanced at the screen, stunned to see it was after ten. "What's up?"

"My brother got himself in hot water and needs a lawyer."

As legal counsel for the Invincibles, I'd also agreed to provide the same for their family members.

"Where is he?"

Vex hesitated. "Vegas lockup."

"Bail?"

"Not set. He goes before a judge tomorrow afternoon."

"What's he in for?"

"Counting cards—"

"That's not illegal unless he used some kind of external device or had an accomplice." I realized I'd interrupted him. "Sorry, go ahead with what you were going to say."

Vex sighed. "That's not what he's in for."

I leaned up against the porch railing. "What *is* he in for?" I asked, wishing he'd just get to the point.

"He was arrested for felony assault."

"The weapon?"

"A gun."

Nevada was an open carry state, but that didn't mean taking one into a casino was permitted. The way the law was worded, it was illegal to take a loaded firearm into any public place where signs prohibiting firearms were posted at each public entrance. Something I was relatively certain all casinos made standard practice.

"He didn't have a CCW permit."

CCW, or carrying a concealed weapon, without a permit *was* illegal in Nevada.

"Anything else I need to know?"

"The security guy he assaulted is still in surgery."

"Got it."

"I don't want the Invincibles posting bail, Fury. I'll take care of whatever it is."

"Understood. One more question, Vex. Where are you now?"

"DFW, trying to get a flight out."

"Since the appearance isn't until tomorrow afternoon, I'll catch a flight in the morning."

Vex said he'd let me know if he heard anything more about the condition of the security guard his brother had assaulted, and we ended the call. When I opened the door to go back inside, Tres was on his way out.

"Is everything okay?" he asked.

"A client needs me to attend a hearing in Las Vegas on behalf of his brother."

"When?"

"Tomorrow afternoon. I'll fly out in the morning." I looked at my phone again, even though I already knew how late it was. "We should probably leave soon." Before I could step over the threshold, my cell rang with another call from Vex. "I need to take this, but I'll come in when I'm done," I said to Tres, who nodded and shut the door behind him.

"Hey, Vex."

"The security guard died." I could tell he had a hard time getting the words out.

"Understood. I'll let you know when my flight is scheduled to land."

"We'll leave in the morning," I heard Tres say when I ended the call and went inside.

"Sorry, everyone, but I should probably call it a night. I guess Tres told you I have to travel to Las Vegas tomorrow."

My mom walked over and took my hands in hers. "Is there anything you need us to do, sweetheart?" she asked.

I leaned forward and kissed her cheek. "Thanks, Mom, but I'll be okay. I probably won't be there for longer than a day or two."

"Let us know if anything changes. I'm glad Tres is going with you."

I started to tell her he wasn't, but decided it wasn't worth the drama that might ensue. Instead, I thanked my sister and her husband, kissed my niece, nephew, and father, and Tres and I left.

"Why did my mom say she was glad you were going with me?" I asked once we were on the road.

"Because I am."

"Tres—"

"I'm going with you, Ellison."

"I'm leaving in the morning."

"I know."

"But you have to work."

Tres shook his head. "I already contacted Maeve to tell her I will be unable to work tomorrow or this weekend."

"Tres, I hardly need an escort to Las Vegas. Plus, my client is flying out tonight. If I need him to, he can pick me up at the airport, or I can catch a car service."

He reached over and held my hand. "It is settled, *mi tormenta*. I'm going with you."

Rather than continuing to argue in the car, I waited until we returned to my place before letting my anger loose.

"You need to leave, Tres. Tonight. Now, in fact."

He walked over to where I stood in the kitchen with my arms folded, and put his hands on my shoulders. "Tell me why you are angry."

I took a step back and jerked my body so his hands fell away. "I told you I didn't want you to go with me, and you ignored me."

He raised his head, looked up at the ceiling, then closed his eyes. After a few seconds, he opened them and looked into mine. "I am sorry."

As mad as I was, I was stunned when I felt the anger dissipate. "I still think you should leave."

"I will, but first, I beg you to allow me to explain."

7

Tres

I breathed a sigh of relief when Ellison finally nodded, walked over to the sofa, and motioned for me to join her. "I'm listening," she said when I sat beside her.

"There are days I look in the mirror and see my father's image reflected back at me. Tonight, it was his voice I heard instead." As much as I wanted to hold her in my arms, I leaned forward and put my head in my hands. "I promise you I meant no disrespect."

"Tres, I doubt you know this, but before I became a lawyer, I worked for the CIA. Believe me when I say traveling to Las Vegas alone will not be a problem for me."

I nodded. "I understand."

"Do you? Really?"

I turned to look into her eyes. "I do. I promise."

She reached for my hand and pulled me closer to her. When I wrapped my arms around her, Ellison rested her head on my shoulder.

"That has to be some kind of record," I heard her say.

"What do you mean?"

"I was really mad at you."

I put my fingers on her chin and lifted her face so I could see her expression. "I know."

"And now I'm not."

"I'm very happy to hear it." I rested against the sofa, and Ellison shifted so her head was on my chest. "What I'm about to say may make you angry again, though."

"Go ahead, Tres."

"I don't want to leave. If we're going to be apart, I want to hold you in my arms tonight. I cannot bear the thought of not making love to you."

"Well, if you can't bear it, I suppose I can handle one more night of the best sex I've ever had." She looked up at me and winked.

While she was teasing, I sensed the idea of me leaving, left her feeling as unsettled as I was. Part of me knew it would have been easier if I did. As it was, when she returned from Las Vegas, it was unlikely I'd still be in Texas.

8

Fury

The gentle and sweet way Tres made love to me almost brought me to tears. Rather than feeling as though we'd only be apart for a couple of days, it felt as though it was the last time I'd see him.

I couldn't believe I actually considered telling him I'd changed my mind and wanted him to come to Las Vegas with me when the feeling of dread I'd experienced on our run returned full force.

"Tres?" I whispered as we lay in bed, my back to his front, hoping if he was asleep, I wouldn't wake him.

"Yes, *mi amor*?"

I smiled. "Is everything okay? I mean between us?"

He tightened his arms around me. "It is more than okay."

I looked over my shoulder. "Are you sure?"

When Tres reached up and turned on the light, I rolled over so I was facing him. "What is bothering you?" he asked.

"I have a bad feeling. Right here." I brought my fist to my heart.

He put his hand around my wrist and brought my clenched hand to his lips. "Ellison, I need to—"

I released my fingers and touched his lips with their tips. "Wait. Don't say anything else. I changed my mind. I want you to come with me."

He studied me. "Are you certain?"

"Yes. I really want you to."

He closed his eyes like he had earlier, before he begged me to let him explain. "Okay," he said, opening his eyes and looking into mine.

I knew I should ask what he was going to tell me when I stopped him. But just thinking about it, made the bad feeling return.

Rather than having to arrange for a commercial flight, Hammer called the next morning to say one of the Invincibles' planes was waiting at the airfield at Austin-Bergstrom.

"It's one of the perks of the job, Fury," Hammer said when I thanked him. "Get used to it."

I wasn't sure I ever would, but given it meant we didn't need to check bags or go through security at the main terminal, I was happy to make use of the private jet.

Hammer also arranged for a car service to pick us up so neither Tres nor I needed to leave a vehicle at the airfield.

While I doubted I'd ever get accustomed to traveling in something as luxurious as the Invincibles' plane, Tres appeared unfazed by it. At least until I introduced him to the pilot.

"Tres Barello, meet Crash Lavery and his copilot, Angel Evans."

Tres looked from me to Crash, then at me again. As hard as I tried not to laugh, I couldn't hold it in. His eyes lit up. "Oh, you're teasing."

Crash shook his head. "Sadly, she's not. As you can see, I'm still in one piece, which means I haven't crashed an airplane."

"Yet," said Angel, winking at Tres and me.

When we took our seats, Tres crossed himself, then kissed me.

"Are you religious?"

"Usually, no, but given our pilot's name, I figured a prayer and kiss for good luck was in order."

"I liked the kiss part." I leaned in for another.

"We'll be in the air for approximately three hours," Angel said from the cockpit before shutting the cabin door. "There's a stateroom in the plane's aft, if you're inclined to use it. Just wait until we reach cruising altitude. You'll hear three chimes when we have, then you're free to move about."

As much as I wanted to spend the next three hours in the stateroom's bed with Tres, I couldn't afford the distraction. The arrest report for Kruger Dunning, Vex's brother, had been uploaded, and I needed to review it before we got in front of the judge this afternoon.

"What's bothering you?" Tres asked when I let out a heavy sigh.

"There's no mention of a gun," I mumbled. "I've read through this document several times, and there isn't a single report of a gun."

He studied me but didn't say anything.

"That's why he was arrested. Aggravated assault. Well, Vex said felony assault, but assault with a deadly weapon falls under the aggravated category. Since the security guard he allegedly assaulted died, I'm anticipating the charges will escalate to murder. At best, manslaughter. But without the gun, there's no reason for the arrest in the first place. Counting cards isn't illegal, as much as the casinos wish it was." I knew I was rambling. Sometimes speaking out loud helped me figure out things that made no sense. Unfortunately, that wasn't the case now.

I sent a message to Vex, asking if he'd been able to speak with his brother either last night or this morning.

"You are thinking he's being framed," Tres said when I set my phone down.

"Gut reaction? Yes, that's exactly what I'm thinking. Why, though?" My question was rhetorical, but Tres seemed to be deep in thought over it.

"You mentioned counting cards. If he's good at it, perhaps the casino owners wished to have him arrested by any means possible."

"I was thinking the same thing. This seems extreme, though. I mean, they could just ban him. That happens all the time."

"Perhaps it's personal."

I nodded. It was the only logical explanation I'd come up with thus far. Although I hadn't. Tres had.

"There is one other consideration."

"What's that?" I asked.

"If he's won a significant amount of money."

"Another good point."

I read through the report twice more, mentioning certain things contained in it to Tres. Nothing else was as significant as the gun.

Once we'd landed, I checked my phone, but I hadn't received a response from Vex. Given I'd told him I'd let him know when we arrived, I called rather than send another message.

"Hey, Fury. I was just about to respond to your question. Sorry for the delay, but I was hoping to talk to my brother before I replied. I haven't been able to, though."

"Are you at the detention center now?" I asked.

"I am."

"I'll head directly there."

Vex thanked me before ending the call.

"I'm sorry about this," I said to Tres. "You can check into the hotel if you'd like."

He shook his head. "I would much prefer to accompany you."

I found the discrepancies in this case increasingly troubling, so Tres would get no argument about going with me.

The seven-mile drive took over thirty minutes since there was no getting around the Las Vegas traffic—at least according to the driver of the car service. When I felt sure we'd been around the same block more than once, I squeezed Tres' hand and looked out the window on my side of the car, then out the other. He squeezed mine after doing the same thing.

The next time the car stopped at a traffic light and we were four cars back from the intersection as well as in the middle lane, conveniently surrounded by semis, I saw Tres grip the door handle with one hand while he grabbed both our bags with the other. When he opened the door and jumped out, I was right behind him.

We darted in and out of the stopped traffic, through one door of a coffeehouse, then out the other, then into a shopping center. Once I was certain we weren't being followed, I called Vex.

"Where are you?" was the first thing he said when he answered my call. There was a frantic edge to his voice.

"Near the intersection of Charleston and Smith—"

"Do not attempt to come to the detention center," he said before I had the chance to tell him about our strange experience.

"What's going on, Vex?"

"There was an attempt on my brother's life about thirty minutes ago. The entire place is on lockdown."

"What's his present condition?" I asked.

"He's in the infirmary, but his injuries are not believed to be life-threatening."

"Vex, do you believe Kruger is safe where he is now?"

"I'm not certain."

"I reviewed the arrest report, and there isn't a single mention of the deadly weapon your brother was alleged to have in his possession. I've already begun preparing a motion to dismiss."

"I need to get him the fuck out of Las Vegas."

I concurred, but I wasn't certain of the fastest way to make that happen, outside of him being taken into federal custody.

"Have you been in contact with McKenna Walsh?" The woman, whose code name was Scottie, had been undercover with Vex on a recent mission involving infiltrating the Aryan Brotherhood of Texas.

At the time of the mission, she'd been on loan from the Department of Homeland Security. I'd recently heard the FBI hired her out from under DHS. I knew from the hot wash—or after-action briefing—that prior to the FBI swooping in, Vex had been pushing for the Invincibles to make her an offer.

"She's on her way as we speak. Or will be."

I raised a brow, not that Vex could see me. "When is she scheduled to arrive?"

"I ended the call with her when yours came in. She said she'd get on the road as soon as she could. I doubt there will be a hearing this afternoon anyway. I'm sorry about this, Fury."

"Nothing to apologize for. This is my job. Tell me, is her intention to have Kruger taken into FBI custody?"

"If she can make it happen."

"Does she have the clout to do it?"

"I don't know."

"Understood. I'll check in with Hammer and see what he recommends."

I looked up and saw Tres was also on his phone. Maybe he'd called Hammer, since he worked for him too.

"Where did you say you were?" Vex asked.

"Long story, but I have a feeling the driver of the car service that picked me up may have a connection to whoever tried to kill your brother."

"Jesus," he muttered under his breath.

"I'm going to work on finding somewhere else to stay. If my suspicions are right and the driver was intentionally trying to keep me from getting to the detention center, or worse, it means whoever he works for likely knows where we planned to stay as well."

"We?"

"Someone came with me. His name is Tres."

"Tres from the Long Branch?" Vex asked.

"Yes."

Vex didn't ask any more questions, and I didn't offer any explanation.

By the time my call ended, Tres was off his.

"I have arranged for another place to stay," he said.

"Okay. Um, thanks."

"Someone I know will meet us here and take us to the house."

"House?"

Tres nodded.

No one would dispute the fact I was a control freak. Including me. Having Tres by my side, though, made me feel safe. His quick thinking when we'd jumped out of the car had impressed me. While it was hard for me not to grill him about where we were staying or who was picking us up, I came to the realization I trusted him.

"What are you thinking, *mi tormenta*?"

"How glad I am you're with me."

His face broke into a broad smile. "Your saying so humbles me."

It was the second time he'd said something to that effect, and it was another thing I liked about him. The list was rapidly growing.

"He's here," Tres said a few minutes later. He led me out a side entrance, where a black SUV with heavily tinted windows waited. "Meet my friend Alejandro," he said after we climbed into the backseat.

"Please forgive me for not exiting the vehicle. It is a pleasure to meet you."

The man's accent was similar to Tres', and while I wondered how they knew each other, I didn't ask.

We drove about twenty minutes outside the city and through the gates of what looked like a high-end community. The place Alejandro pulled into was one of the nicer I'd seen as he drove through the neighborhood.

"Welcome to *La Casa del Atardecer del Desierto*," he said after pulling into one of the four garages, and we exited the vehicle. He waved us inside the modern house, where it was clear no expense had been spared.

"Like the street it resides on, this place was named for the fabulous views of the desert sunset," he said as he led us past a chef's dream kitchen and over to one of two glass garage-style doors that opened to panoramic views. "What you see is known as the Red Rock Conservation Area. No other homes can be built on it for one hundred years."

He opened the second, which led to an outdoor living area as large as the indoor great room. Beyond the seating and bar areas were an infinity pool and spa. So far, I'd counted four fireplaces, two of which were outside, and we hadn't seen any of the bedrooms yet.

"I will deliver your bags to the west suite if you'd like."

"Please," Tres responded.

"This place is unbelievable," I whispered once Alejandro left us on our own.

Tres nodded but appeared nonplussed by our lavish surroundings as he gave me a tour.

When we returned to the main room, he stood behind me and put his arms around my waist. I looked out at the perfectly appointed xeriscaping.

"Later, we will make use of the pool," he said as he trailed kisses down my neck.

"I didn't bring a suit."

Tres nipped my shoulder. "I wouldn't have allowed you to wear one if you had."

I glanced at him over my shoulder. "What about your friend?"

"He will not be here this evening."

I leaned back so my head rested against his chest. "Thank you, Tres, for coming with me and for making arrangements for us to stay here."

"Alejandro is my most trusted associate."

It was odd that he'd used the word associate over friend, but I once again found myself "letting go," as Rip had suggested I attempt to do more often. There was a freedom in doing so that I was beginning to enjoy. However, this was not a pleasure trip, and there were things I needed to take care of.

"I should make a few calls."

Tres squeezed me, then dropped his arms. "Is there anything I can do to help?"

My first inclination was to tell him there wasn't, but maybe there were. "Do you or Alejandro have any connections in Las Vegas, particularly at the casino where the alleged card counting and assault occurred? It's called the Starlight."

"I will inquire."

It had been forty minutes since I last spoke with Vex, so when Tres left to find his friend, I placed another call to him.

"Any update?" I asked when he answered.

"I'm in the infirmary with Kruger now," he responded.

"How is he?"

"He'll be fine. He has a superficial knife wound that needed to be stitched up, but it didn't do any internal damage."

"Is he coherent enough to tell you what happened?"

"He's still groggy, but the doctor said he should be fully alert in about an hour."

"What about Scottie? Have you heard from her about your brother being taken into federal custody?"

"She's still working on it."

I remembered I'd told Vex I'd check in with Hammer and hadn't yet. After reiterating I would, we ended our call, and I placed another.

When he answered, I gave Hammer the rundown of everything that had happened thus far, including my suspicions about the car service and the attempt on Kruger's life. "Scottie Walsh is on her way to Las Vegas," I added. "I'm not sure she has the clout to take Kruger into FBI custody. What kind of connections do the Invincibles have that might be able to assist?"

"Quite a few, and I'll handle it," Hammer offered before asking if there was anything else he needed to know before he started making contact. Part of me wondered if I should tell him Tres had come with me, although maybe Hammer already knew since Tres had spoken to Maeve and told her he wouldn't be able to work tonight or this weekend.

After ending the conversation with Hammer, I sat on one of the outdoor sofas and waited for Tres to return.

"Alejandro said he knows people who work at the Starlight. He's reaching out now." He sat beside me.

"Hammer is working on getting Kruger released to the FBI."

I rested against the sofa and leaned into him when he put his arm around my shoulders. I couldn't remember a time in my life when I felt as comfortable with another person as I did with Tres. Maybe with my family, but that was different. Outside of them, I'd never experienced the calm that settled over me when I was in his arms with anyone. I rested my head on Tres' shoulder, almost falling asleep as he wove his fingers into my hair and gently massaged my scalp. "You are so good to me," I murmured.

"I am good *for* you, Ellison."

"That too. I was just thinking that, other than my parents and sister, no one has ever made me feel as at peace as you do."

"You make me feel the same way."

I found that hard to believe and shifted so I could see his face. "The balance of care here is hardly equal," I said, wishing it sounded more like a joke than it did.

Tres cupped my cheek. "You are wrong, *mi tormenta*. You bring me great joy. I feel as though every choice I've made in my life was all about finding you."

I considered attempting another joke about why he called me a "powerful storm," but he sounded so serious I decided against it. "Do you really mean that?" I asked instead, staring into his eyes.

"With all my heart."

"Maybe it was more about me finding you," I whispered, stunning myself again at how easy the admission of my feelings was when it came to Tres.

He leaned down to kiss me, but neither of us closed our eyes. "We are destined to be together, Ellison," he said against my lips.

"Are we?" I whispered.

He looked up at the sky and closed his eyes like I'd seen him do more than once. When his gaze returned to mine, I could feel the weight of his emotion. "When I think about you being in danger," he shook his head. "It fills me with a fear like I've never known." He gripped the back of my neck. "You may say I'm *loco*—crazy— but the way I feel about you…the way I've felt since I saw you for the first time…" His voice trailed off.

"When you asked me to dance?"

"No, *mi amor*, it was before that. Sometimes, it seems like it was a dream, but I remember the first night you came into the Long Branch. You took my breath away, but not just because of your beauty. It was as though I knew you. I *felt* your presence. Crazy, yes?"

"Not crazy."

Tres raised a brow.

"You may find this hard to believe, but the way I am with you, I'm not like this with *anyone* else."

"It is easy for me to believe since it is the same for me."

It was my turn to raise a brow.

Tres chuckled. "It is true. Ask Alejandro." The smile left Tres' face. "What I'm about to say may 'freak you out,' as the American expression goes, but I want to marry you, Ellison. Today. Right now. I want you to be mine and for me to be yours. No matter what happens."

One word I'd never believed would be used to describe me was "rash." Except, right now, it's all I wanted to be.

"You do not appear horrified," he said, his voice barely above a whisper.

"Because I'm not."

"Tell me why, Ellison."

I tried to look away, but he wouldn't release his grasp on the back of my neck.

"Tell me," he repeated.

"What if it horrifies *you*?"

"Nothing you say could. Unless it is that you don't want to be with me."

"I…" I couldn't bring myself to say the words. It seemed so ridiculous, so impossible.

"I feel the same way," he said, resting his forehead against mine.

"It's nuts—*loco*," I whispered.

"Do you trust me?"

I leaned back so I could look into his eyes again. "I do."

9

Tres

I hadn't lied when I said Ellison brought me great joy. The way I felt when I looked into her eyes was indescribable. Perhaps it wasn't just joy. Love is what I felt, and I knew, no matter what the next few weeks brought, I had to do everything in my power to settle things with my family—my father—once and for all, so I could spend the rest of my life with the woman who owned my heart.

Thus, I couldn't risk waiting for us to marry. I had to bind her to me so when I was finished doing the hardest thing I'd ever been faced with, she would still be mine.

"Do you remember me saying I had a horrible feeling?" She took my hand and put it on her heart. "Right here?"

"I do." The guilt I felt then and now nearly consumed me.

"I couldn't face the idea we'd be apart. It's why I changed my mind and asked you to come with me."

"I am so grateful you did."

She smiled. "Don't be. It was purely selfish on my part."

Her mobile rang, jarring us both from one of the most important conversations we could have.

"I'm sorry, but I need to take this."

"Of course." I released her from my arms, and she stood.

"Hey, Hammer," I heard her say, followed by several seconds of silence. "That's great news. Thank you."

Ellison returned to the sofa where she'd been sitting. "Hammer was able to arrange for Vex's brother to be taken into FBI custody. Which means there won't be a hearing this afternoon. Or ever. Las Vegas will no longer have jurisdiction over his case. Since an agent is already en route, she'll be able to make the necessary arrangements." Her eyes scrunched. "I need to be there, though, just in case LVPD tries to fight it."

"There is the matter of your safety. I will have Alejandro provide private security to escort us."

"The Invincibles will reimburse the expense."

"Do not concern yourself with that at this time."

"Thank you, Tres."

I kissed her once more, then excused myself to find Alejandro.

"I need your assistance," I said to him in Spanish, our native language.

"Of course."

I explained Ellison and I would need a security escort to the detention center. Once finished there, the same security would accompany us to the marriage licensing bureau. After we obtained the license, Ellison and I could be wed in any of the chapels located on or near the Las Vegas Strip.

"I will file the necessary documentation online since I already have a copy of Ms. Storm's identification."

I nodded and left the room, anxious to return to Ellison. I panicked momentarily when I didn't see her, but breathed a sigh of relief when I found her sitting on the pool's edge, dangling her feet in the water.

"I couldn't resist," she said when I knelt beside her.

"Would you like to go for a swim?"

"What about your friend?" she asked a second time.

"He knows better than to disturb us."

Ellison raised a brow, making me realize perhaps my statement had been worded too strongly.

"After I send him a message asking for privacy," I added.

"While you do that, I'll call Vex and give him an update."

I walked a short distance from her and sent a text to Alejandro, not that it would be necessary. As I'd originally said, he knew better than to disturb us unless I called for him.

"We have two hours," Ellison said when she ended her call and returned to where I waited.

"Remove your clothes, *mi amor*." I walked over and sat on a chaise I'd moved closer to the pool.

"Aren't you going in with me?" she asked, pouting.

"I will be."

"Then, why aren't you undressing?"

"I want to see what is mine, my love." I stood and walked over to her. "You are mine, aren't you, Ellison?"

"I am, Tres."

"Show me."

Ellison slowly unfastened the buttons of her blouse, then slid it off her shoulders. I held out my hand, and she gave it to me.

"Trousers next, but leave your panties on."

She raised a brow but unfastened her slacks, slowly like she had her blouse. She kicked off her heels and stepped out of her clothes. When I held my hand out a second time, she gave them to me.

"Turn around and face the pool."

When she did, I took my time folding her clothing and setting it on a table before I stood, walked over, and laid two towels down, one at the edge of the pool. I stood behind her, close enough that she could lean against me before I reached around and cupped her breasts. I captured both nipples with my fingers through the lace of her bra, gradually increasing the pressure until Ellison moaned.

"Can you feel how much I want you?" I whispered, grinding my hardness against her ass.

When she whimpered, I let go and eased both hands into her panties. I thrust two fingers into her heat while I used my other hand to play with her clit. Within mere moments, Ellison climaxed.

"Sit on the towel on the edge of the pool," I said after pulling her panties down to her ankles and she stepped out. "Leave your bra on."

Without turning around to look at me, Ellison followed my instructions to the letter.

While her back was still to me, I removed my clothing and used the steps to her left to walk into the pool. Once in front of her, I spread her legs, using my hands to part her folds.

"Reach down and play with your clit, *mi tormenta*." When she hesitated, I leaned forward and captured her nipple between my teeth, slowly increasing the bite until she moaned. "Play with your clit, Ellison," I repeated, moving my mouth to her other breast. Before I could capture her a second time, I felt her reach between our bodies. I backed away and watched as she pinched herself with her thumb and forefinger.

"Now, your other hand." This time, she didn't hesitate. "Make yourself come." I held her open and watched as she put two fingers into her pussy while her other hand continued working her clit.

I could tell she was on the edge when Ellison closed her eyes and tilted her head back.

I quickly nipped at the side of her breast. "Open your eyes and watch," I demanded.

By then, her mewls of pleasure had me on the edge too. I moved her hands away, pulled her closer to the water, and thrust inside her. She wrapped her arms around my neck as I moved her pussy up and down on my cock, then stopped. Her eyes sprung open.

"I am not wearing a condom, *mi amor*. Tell me now if you want me to stop."

She answered by attempting to lower her pussy onto me, but I held her still. "I want to come inside you."

"I'm on birth control," she said, loosening her arms from around my neck.

I lifted her from the deck, and she wrapped her legs around my waist. With my hands holding her ass, I increased my tempo until we both cried out in pleasure.

I continued to hold her until the spasms of her pussy stopped. Then I walked us both to the pool's edge, eased myself from her warmth, and set her on the towel.

"Keep your legs spread," I said, reaching around to unfasten her bra. "I am not finished with you."

Ellison gasped and wrapped her arms around me, pulling me close as if she wanted to hide her body with mine.

"Mis disculpas, pero es urgente que hable contigo," I heard Alejandro behind me, saying he was sorry for interrupting, but there was an urgent matter we needed to discuss.

In anger, I lifted myself out of the pool, wrapped one towel around Ellison, and held out my hand to help her stand. "Wait for me inside."

I grabbed the second towel and stalked toward him. "What did you see?"

He held up both hands. *"No vi nada. Lo juro."*

After he swore he didn't see anything, I asked what was so urgent that he'd ignore my direct order.

"Recibí un mensaje de La Pequeña Gorrión."

"You heard from the Little Sparrow? What about?"

"Tu padre."

I put my hands on my hips and rolled my shoulders. "My father? How much time do we have?"

"Tenemos que irnos lo antes posible."

If we needed to leave as soon as possible, it had to mean my father had found me.

10

Fury

While Tres acted as if nothing had happened, I could feel the tension in his body when he embraced me and apologized.

"Did he learn something about what happened at the Starlight with Vex's brother?"

"Not specifically, but he believes he may have a lead on who arranged for the car service that picked us up at the airport."

"If it's just a lead, why was it urgent he speak with you?" I asked as I rushed to put my clothes on.

"Alejandro tends to be…dramatic."

"You said he wouldn't interrupt us."

"I am sorry, my love. I can assure you he didn't see anything."

"Meaning what?"

He wrapped his arm around me and nuzzled my neck. "He did not see the way I made love to you or the look on your face *cuando tuviste un orgasmo*."

"We should probably head to the detention center soon anyway. Will Alejandro still be able to take us there?"

"Of course. He has also arranged for the additional security we spoke of earlier."

"Good." My hands were shaking so much it was taking me twice as long to button my blouse.

"Let me, *mi tormenta*," said Tres, resting his hands on mine. "Has Alejandro upset you this much?"

"No. I mean, yes. I don't know. It isn't like I really care much about stuff like that."

Tres' eyes opened wide.

"Please don't misunderstand. I wouldn't want anyone watching us. I'm just not a prude, ya know?"

"What can I do to help you relax again?"

I closed my eyes and settled into his touch when he began rubbing my shoulders.

"Come with me, Ellison."

I didn't know where we were going, but if more back rubs were involved, I'd follow happily. The man had magic hands, and not just for massages.

"We have time to shower," he said after leading me into a bedroom that seemed bigger than my entire house. As I looked around, somewhat stunned, Tres helped me out of my clothes before removing his own.

"I really loved my bathroom," I said when he led me into the en suite.

"Why do you say it that way?" he asked as he pressed several buttons on a wall panel outside a shower that looked big enough to hold a party in.

I waved my hands around. "Look at this place. It's…I can't even think of an appropriate word to describe it. Palatial, maybe."

Tres took both my hands in his and brought them to his lips. "I still love your bathroom. It will always be my favorite in the whole world."

I rolled my eyes. "After this one."

"No other compares." He shook his head and led me into the king-size shower. As he soothed me with the most amazingly scented body wash I'd ever smelled, he told me how much he loved the curve of my spine, the dimples above my buttocks, the back of my knees, and the soft skin under my breasts. I clung to him when the headiness of his words made me swoon.

"Sit," he said, leading me over to one of the benches built into each side of the space. When I sat, he knelt in front of me. I expected him to spread my legs when he rested the palms of his hands on my knees, but he didn't.

"Ellison, earlier I said I want to marry you. I'm asking you now. Will you make me the happiest man alive and become my wife? Will you marry me?"

I put my hands on top of his and stared into his eyes. "You're serious, aren't you?"

"I have never been more serious about anything in my life."

"Tres…I don't know what to say."

He leaned forward, resting his chest against my legs and his hands on either side of my hips. "Have you ever felt this way before in your life? Do you not believe, as I do, that our souls are already one?"

I shook my head. "No, I've never felt anything close to how I feel when I'm with you. I thought I did once, but now I know how wrong I was. Does it mean our souls are already one? I don't know how to respond to that."

"You said you experienced a bad feeling when you thought about us being apart."

"I did."

"When we ran from the car, all I could think about was how I never would have forgiven myself if I hadn't come to Las Vegas and something had happened to you. My heart ached just thinking I may have lost you. I can't lose you, Ellison. Do you understand? I *can't*. My heart would break into a million pieces."

"Tres…"

"Tell me how you feel, *mi tormenta*. If you don't believe we are meant to be together the way I do, I will accept it. I will be brokenhearted, but I will respect whatever you say."

My mind raced with all the reasons I should tell him it was too soon, that we hardly knew each other, or that it was impossible to fall in love with someone in a matter of days. But I couldn't say any of those things, because like Tres, I did believe we were meant to be together. The idea that we wouldn't be, made my heart hurt like it never had before, even when I realized the man I once thought I'd marry had betrayed me.

I took a deep breath and let it out slowly. "Yes."

"Yes?" Tres stood and pulled me up with him. "Yes, you will marry me?"

"Yes, I will marry you."

He picked me up and spun me around in the water streaming from the shower heads on all sides of us. It felt as though we were in the middle of a fountain during a rainstorm. And when Tres kissed me, I knew it was the absolute most romantic and most wonderful moment of my life. I knew in the deepest recesses of my heart that this was how it felt to truly be in love with someone. As Tres said, our souls were already one.

"Ellison—"

I reached up and kissed him. This time, I wanted to be the one to speak. I put my hands on either side of his face and stared into his eyes. "I love you, Tres."

"Say it again," he whispered.

"I love you."

"And I love you, my beautiful, amazing, powerful, and perfect storm."

11

Fury

In the hours following Tres' proposal, he and I arrived at the Las Vegas Detention Center at the same time as Scottie Walsh. Shortly thereafter, Kruger Dunning was released into her custody without any pushback from LVPD.

Once we'd gotten that out of the way, she, Vex, Kruger, Alejandro, and four other men, to whom I hadn't been formally introduced, accompanied Tres and me first to the Clark County Marriage License Bureau, then across the street to the Viva Las Vegas Wedding Chapel. After a fifteen-minute ceremony performed by none other than an ordained Elvis impersonator, we were pronounced man and wife.

Now five of us—Tres, Vex, Scottie, Kruger, and me—were on the Invincibles' plane, flown by Crash and Angel, headed back to Texas.

Given this was our "wedding night," Tres and I took Angel's suggestion of retiring to the stateroom after all but the pilot and copilot shared a bottle of champagne.

Since my only role in Kruger's case had been to appear as his legal counsel in Las Vegas, there would be plenty of time tomorrow, or even next week, for Vex to brief me on exactly what had led to his brother's arrest. I highly doubted there would be further charges pressed, given, in my opinion, the entire thing seemed like a setup.

Whether Kruger was still in any kind of danger as a result of what had taken place at the Starlight Casino was another question entirely. One that, thankfully, would be handled by the Invincibles team without any help from me.

Part of me had expected a pushback from Vex when I told him where we were headed after his brother's release. Instead, he'd expressed sincere happiness for Tres and me and offered to serve as a witness at the ceremony if we needed one.

As I lay in Tres' arms on the bed in the plane's stateroom, I felt happier than I ever had at any time in my life. Happier than when I graduated from law school, than when I passed the bar, and when Hammer asked me to join his firm and take over as the legal counsel for the Invincibles.

I'd been thrilled for my sister when she married Jimmy and when my niece then nephew were born, but what I felt tonight was my own joyousness—and Tres'.

I thought about Hammer and Maeve, Rip and Pearl, and some of the other Invincibles partners and their wives and how skeptical I'd been when they seemed to fall madly in love in a relatively short period of time. Or when their newfound love took precedence over seemingly everything else in their lives. Now, though, I completely understood their over-the-top giddiness because I felt it myself.

While a tiny part of me was curious about what had happened with Kruger, ninety-nine percent of me couldn't have cared less. Especially after Tres and I made love, then spent the rest of the flight talking about where we'd travel on our honeymoon.

"Tomorrow, we will get our wedding rings," Tres said when we'd landed in Austin and were on our way to my house. I supposed, soon, it would be our house, unless Tres wanted to live somewhere else. As happy as I felt, I didn't care where we lived, and I said so.

"I have already told you your bathroom is my favorite on earth," he said, kissing me as we rode in the backseat of a car service not unlike the one we'd ridden in, in Las Vegas. "Your bed is too."

"*Our* bed."

"You have made me the happiest man alive," Tres said when we arrived at the house and he carried me over the threshold.

He'd just kicked the door closed when my work cell rang. As much as I wanted to ignore it, I knew I couldn't. When I'd accepted the Invincibles job, Hammer warned me I would be on call twenty-four hours a day, seven days a week, for as long as I remained in their employ. At the time, it seemed like a no-brainer, given the amount of my retainer. Now, though, I dreaded what the call might mean.

"Hey, Fury, I'm sorry to bug you, but I wanted to make sure you received the message from Hammer, saying he wants us to meet him at the Hammered Dubliner tomorrow at zero eight hundred. The message said it was urgent IISG business."

"Zero eight hundred? Are you kidding me, Vex? Did you tell him I just got *married*?"

"I didn't think it was my place. I'm sorry. Do you want me to call him?"

I sighed. "No." I wouldn't call him, either. Again, this was what I'd signed up for. Hammer had always been good to me, and he deserved to hear that Tres and I were married from me and in person.

"I'm sorry," I said after reiterating to Tres what Vex had told me.

"Don't be. While I don't know all of what IISG does, I do know some. I prefer the acronym, by the way."

IISG stood for the Invincible Intelligence and Security Group, and as Tres said, the acronym was certainly better than always referring to them as the Invincibles.

"I'd love for you to come with me, but since Vex said this is an urgent matter, I don't think it would be a good idea."

Tres kissed the back of my left hand, stopping at the third finger. "While you are meeting, I will buy your wedding ring. Unless you would prefer to pick it out yourself."

I shook my head. "If you choose it, it will mean so much more."

As much as I wanted Tres and me to make love all night, both of us were exhausted and quickly fell to sleep. When the alarm rang at zero six hundred, I kissed him and insisted he stay in bed.

"Jewelry stores don't open for another four hours. Maybe I'll be back before then and we can go together. Better yet, why don't you wait for me right here, and we can consummate our marriage all over again?"

"I like the sound of that best," Tres murmured as his eyes drifted closed.

When I walked in the front door of Hammer's house an hour later, I was stunned to see Decker Ashford and Keon Edgemon seated at the main dining room table. Vex and Rip were there as well.

"Am I late?" I asked, setting my bag on the floor, next to an open seat.

"Not at all. They were all early," said Hammer, pushing back from his chair and standing like the rest of the men in the room had. "You look like you could use a cup of coffee."

"Um, thanks, I think." I looked around the room. "Gentlemen, please be seated. I'm just one of the guys at these meetings."

Hammer laughed and disappeared into the kitchen. Before he returned, my questioning eyes met Vex's, and he shook his head. I assumed that meant he hadn't mentioned my nuptials to anyone yet.

Hammer handed me a cup of coffee, and we took our seats.

"Okay with everyone if I give Fury a quick rundown while we're waiting for Agent Walsh?" he asked.

"Go ahead," said Decker while everyone else seated nodded.

"Fury, my apologies for not informing you of this sooner; there were reasons I couldn't."

My eyes scrunched as I waited for him to continue.

"Kruger Dunning was part of an undercover op in Las Vegas. Even Vex was unaware of the exact details and extent of the mission."

"I still am," Vex leaned over and said.

Ashford cleared his throat but didn't speak.

I heard the front door open and turned to see Scottie walk in. "Sorry if I'm late," she said. "I had a little trouble with the gate."

"That was my fault," said Hammer's wife, Maeve, sticking her head out the door between the kitchen and dining room. "My apologies, everyone," she said as she ducked back into the kitchen.

I glanced at Hammer and smiled. The look on his face probably would've turned my stomach—perhaps a slight exaggeration—a week ago, but now, it made me think about Tres, at home in bed, awaiting my return. I imagined the look on my face would be much like Hammer's when I was finally able to rejoin him.

"Let's get started," said Decker, looking at his watch.

Hammer cleared his throat like Decker had a minute ago. I was beginning to think the "old guys" were getting impatient with us young guns. "As I mentioned to Fury a few moments ago, Kruger Dunning was part of an FBI undercover operation in Las Vegas at the time of his 'arrest.' Scottie, do you want to take it from here?" he asked.

"Of course." She opened her laptop. "Six months ago, the bureau received new information regarding the thirty-plus-year-old murder of a former FBI agent. The cold case has been reopened several times over the years. This is the first time there seems to be enough credible evidence to solve the crime. Thanks, in part, to the efforts of Agent Dunning."

Discovering Kruger was an FBI agent stunned me more than the details of the case. Particularly since it appeared Vex was as surprised as I was.

"As you may surmise, we believe law enforcement was involved in the murder, as well as the owners of the Starlight, a family with known ties to the Mafia."

It was only when Scottie turned to look at me that I realized I had been drumming my fingers on the table.

"Sorry," I mumbled. "Bad habit."

Scottie pulled a manila envelope from the bag she'd set on the floor. "I've prepared a brief that goes into greater detail about the case. For now, I'll focus solely on the key points."

I took the briefs from her and passed them around the table.

"Where's my brother?" Vex asked, not bothering to look at the document in front of him. I couldn't blame him for being impatient. I would've been far worse if I'd found out my sister was an agent, unbeknownst to me, and for some reason, I hadn't been at a briefing on a case she was investigating.

"He's at an undisclosed location, but he's safe and receiving medical treatment."

Vex's eyebrows shot up. "What for?"

"Better to take this offline after Scottie has finished," Decker suggested.

"Yes, sir," Vex muttered.

"Go ahead, Scottie." Decker made a motion with his hand.

"The murder victim, former FBI Division Commander George Perkins, reported to the Las Vegas bureau field office on the afternoon of 22 August, 1990, after having had lunch with the head of the FBI's western region. That man, Sean O'Malley, did not return to the office when Perkins did. Instead, he went straight to the airport and boarded a flight to California.

"Shortly after four in the afternoon, Perkins returned to his car, which was on the fifth level of the adjacent parking structure. When he started the engine, a bomb planted under the vehicle exploded. His body was burned beyond recognition, necessitating he be identified by dental records."

"No other fatalities?" I asked.

"Perkins was the only person injured in the blast."

When I nodded, Scottie continued.

"A wide variety of suspects were identified, including Perkins' former brothers-in-law, who, at the time, were the two of three primary shareholders in the Starlight Casino."

I didn't need to read the brief to guess the third was the dead agent, which Scottie quickly confirmed.

"Perkins, the third and majority shareholder, inherited his stake in the casino when his wife passed away after a lengthy battle with cancer. As a side note, Perkins' wife was estranged from her brothers at the time of her death, and according to witness statements, Perkins was unaware of her connection to the Starlight until the reading of a will he didn't know she'd had drawn up."

Scottie then jumped ahead to when the FBI received new information leading them to reopen the investigation.

"Six months ago, the man who had been sheriff at the time of Perkins' murder passed away. Shortly following his death, a witness came forward who claimed he had proof the sheriff had covered up the murder that, according to the same witness, had been arranged by Perkins' brothers-in-law. Another side note is only one of the two brothers is still alive."

"Cause of death of the deceased brother?" I asked after reading the reward for information resulting in a conviction in the murder case was currently valued at a quarter of a million dollars.

"Accidental overdose," Scottie responded. "Two years ago."

It was easy to see where this was going, but like with most crimes, suspicion was one thing. Proving it was another.

"The afternoon before his arrest, Agent Dunning met with the witness, who had proof not just of the deceased sheriff's involvement in the cover-up of the crime, but also implicating the man who currently holds the elected position," said Scottie.

"Who owns the Starlight now?" Vex asked.

"Perkins' only surviving brother-in-law."

"Is there evidence of a connection between him and the current sheriff of Clark County?" I asked.

"Nothing admissible," Scottie responded.

"What about the car service that was supposed to deliver me from the airport to the detention center?"

Scottie nodded. "It appears unrelated."

My eyes met Hammer's. "We'll take that offline as well," I said before either he or Decker had the chance to make the suggestion.

"We believe Agent Dunning's cover was blown, resulting in him being framed for the murder of the now-deceased security guard."

"How close was he to proving the brother-in-law's and current sheriff's connection to the murder?" Vex asked.

"According to both Kruger and his boss, very close," Scottie told him.

Vex nodded but didn't say anything else. My guess was once this meeting was over, he'd ask to be read in on his brother's whereabouts as well as be assigned to the case.

"Is there further information in the brief that needs to be reviewed now?" Decker asked.

When Scottie said there wasn't, he stood, thanked everyone still seated, and walked out. Edge followed. Rip stood too but didn't leave.

My eyes met Hammer's again. "Fury, before you get with Scottie and Vex, there's another matter I need to discuss with you."

I stood when he did, and followed him into the kitchen.

"If this is about—"

"Sorry to interrupt, but Decker, Edge, Rip, and I have other urgent business to attend to, so I need to keep this brief."

"Understood."

"As I said, there's another matter I want to discuss."

"Go ahead."

"Maeve and I have recently learned one of the bouncers at the Long Branch might have an issue with Immigration and Customs Enforcement. It makes no sense, but Rebel said someone from ICE came by, looking for him."

"Who's the bouncer?"

"Leandro Barello. Goes by Tres. Maeve suggested we ask her brother to get involved. I'm sure you understand why I'd much prefer we handle it at our level rather than contacting the director of the Central Intelligence Agency."

While I outwardly chuckled, my mind raced with what this meant. If what Hammer said was true, why hadn't Tres told me he had a problem with immigration himself?

I gripped the back of the chair, steadying myself when adrenaline surged through my bloodstream.

"You okay?" Hammer asked.

"Yeah. Fine. I'll look into it."

"Thanks, Fury. Oh, what were you going to say before I interrupted you?"

"Nothing important. You should head out if Decker and Edge are waiting for you. By the way, is whatever you're meeting about something you'll need me to engage on?"

"No."

"Copy that," I muttered, still gripping the back of the chair.

"You sure you're okay?" he asked again.

"Fine. Just tired." I followed him into the main dining room, where Scottie and Vex appeared to be discussing more of what was in the brief.

"Do you want us to take this meeting elsewhere?" I asked when Hammer and Rip headed in the direction of the front door.

"Nah, you can wrap it up here."

When Vex looked up and our eyes met after Hammer and Rip left, he stood. "Everything okay, Fury?"

"I'm not sure."

"Did you tell Hammer about you and Tres?"

I shook my head. "I didn't have the chance."

Vex continued studying me.

"He asked me to look into a possible immigration matter with a Long Branch employee."

Scottie raised her head as if she'd just realized we were in the midst of a conversation unrelated to the Perkins murder investigation.

Vex's eyes opened wider. "It isn't Tres, is it?" he asked.

"You have no idea how much I wish I could say it wasn't."

"Shit, Fury," Vex groaned. "Are you serious?"

I nodded and looked between him and Scottie. "I, um, need to go. There isn't anything urgent you need to cover with me now, is there?"

"Not urgent," she responded. "We can connect later."

I was relieved to hear it, since I doubted I would've been able to concentrate if there had been something to discuss.

The thirty-minute drive from Hammer's ranch to my house felt more like three hours as I struggled not to jump to any conclusions. I couldn't allow myself to consider, even for a moment, that Tres had convinced me to marry him because he was about to be deported. Not that Hammer had said he was about to be. He'd only said ICE came by the Long Branch, looking for

Tres. To jump to the conclusion he might have was paranoid and ridiculous. I trusted Tres. More, I loved him and he loved me. It would be impossible for him to fake the intensity of what was between us.

Although Blake Howell had done exactly that. I'd believed he loved me too. I'd also believed we would get married and spend the rest of our lives together.

But Tres was nothing like Blake. *Tres loved me,* I reminded myself as I exited the highway and took side streets to my house.

When I pulled into the driveway and didn't see his car, the same feeling of dread I'd experienced twice in the last few days overwhelmed me.

Once inside, I raced into the bedroom, gutted when I saw the belongings he'd been accumulating at my house over the course of the last week were gone like he was. When I felt as though I might pass out from the stress of what was happening, I sat down and put my head between my knees.

I took several deep breaths, trying to keep my anger at bay while I processed through his absence.

Even if Tres *had* married me because of an impending deportation, it made no sense he would just disappear. A marriage alone, particularly a hasty one taking place in a Las Vegas wedding chapel, wouldn't hold any weight with immigration.

It also made no sense he'd turn tail and leave. Tres was one of the strongest men I knew, and that included many CIA agents I'd worked with. If he had used me, which was hard for me to believe, he wouldn't just leave. My gut told me he'd square his shoulders and explain why he hadn't been forthright.

I took my work and personal phones out of my bag and placed a call to him from each, one after the other. Both went directly to voicemail. Since the recording said the inbox was full, I was unable to leave a message. Next, I called Maeve.

"Hello, Fury," she answered. "I'm sorry I wasn't able to speak with you before you left."

"Hammer made me aware that ICE stopped by, looking for your bouncer. I've called Tres and have been unable to reach him. Can you tell me if he's on the schedule to work in the next few days?"

"He is not. He requested several days off, saying he wasn't certain when he'd return. I told him to let me know when he was back, and I'd put him back on the schedule."

"I see."

"I'm aware being gainfully employed will help matters with ICE. Do you need a statement or proof of any kind from me?"

"Not yet, but please go ahead and prepare something, so it's ready if I do need it."

"Thanks, Fury. I know this is outside regular IISG business, but Hammer and I both adore Tres, and he's one of our most reliable and trusted employees. I only wish he felt he could come to us to help if there truly is an issue."

"Are you suggesting there may not be?"

"I'm not certain. All Rebel said was an ICE agent came to the bar yesterday, looking for him."

"Was she able to get a business card?"

"I would assume she did, but I neglected to ask. If so, I'm sure she would've left it in the office."

Since it was still too early for anyone to be at the bar, I told Maeve I'd either call or stop by to get the agent's name and contact information.

"Do you want me to run over there now?" she offered.

"You don't need to do that. I'd like to ask Rebel to tell me everything the agent said to her."

"Understood, and that is an excellent idea."

I ended the call with Maeve and took several deep breaths as I felt anger building in my system.

Why wasn't Tres at my house when I returned? Why weren't any of his belongings here? Why wasn't he answering his phone? None of it made sense.

Conversations Tres and I had had, played on repeat in my brain.

"What are you thinking about?" I'd asked.

"A promise I made." A few seconds later, he'd told me he wouldn't break a vow once made.

A few sentences after that, I'd told him I didn't like surprises.

"You will grow to love them," had been his response.

He was wrong. I didn't love this one at all.

12

Fury

After changing out of the clothes I wore to the meeting at Hammer's ranch, I tried Tres' cell once more before driving over to his place.

I'd been somewhat surprised when we stopped by the first time so he could get a change of clothes. While the house was modest, he'd told me he lived there alone. First, it was quite a distance from the Long Branch, where he worked. Second, rent in Austin was astronomical. That he could afford to live here on his own stunned me.

His car wasn't parked in the driveway or out front, but he could've pulled into the detached garage.

I went to the front door and rang the bell. When no one answered, I peered into the windows, trying not to be so obvious I'd look suspicious. I didn't see anything inside that looked different than when we'd been here together. I walked around back and saw a small window on the side of the detached garage. I stood on my tiptoes, and while I couldn't see much, what I didn't see was a vehicle inside.

I looked in the windows on the back of the house like I had the front with a similar result—it was evident Tres wasn't here.

I cursed myself for not getting Alejandro's number while we were in Las Vegas. Other than that he knew people who worked at the Starlight Casino, I didn't know anything else about the man.

A few things stood out to me when Tres had talked about his friend. First, he'd referred to him as his associate. Something else he'd said led me to believe Tres was somehow the man's boss, which made no sense. Unless…I shook my head and swore under my breath. Unless there was a fuck lot Hammer, Maeve, and I didn't know about Leandro Barello.

While I still knew plenty of people at the CIA and I could easily have asked Hammer for support from the Invincibles' contacts, there were a few things I could check on my own first.

I drove back to my place, hoping, regardless of how ridiculous it was, Tres would be there, waiting for me. While not surprised, I felt my anger build when he wasn't.

I went inside, wishing his scent didn't linger in my small house. I opened all the windows, then changed my mind and closed them. As much as Tres' disappearance infuriated me, it *hurt* more. I wasn't sure I was ready to erase all trace of him yet.

I pulled out my laptop, logged onto IISG's secure server, and began my search.

As it turned out, Leandro Barello was a very common name, even within the State of Texas. Opening the search regionally yielded an equally high number of men with the same name. While Tres had told me he was from Spain, not Mexico, I was beginning to wonder if anything he'd told me was the truth. Including things like his name—and that he loved me.

I slammed my laptop closed in frustration, only to open it seconds later when it occurred to me I might get quicker results from a property search. If I could identify the owner of the house Tres lived in, in Austin, maybe I could find contact information for him or her.

As I quickly learned, and had feared, the deed was in the name of a holding company—*Activos Comerciales de Mallorca LLC*—rather than an individual. The only available contact information was a post office box. Using a simplistic app, I translated the name to

Business Assets of Mallorca. Which, other than nam-ing a region of Spain, was about as vague an entity name as there could be.

I really didn't want to involve Hammer and Maeve—primarily to avoid the humiliation of having to confess I'd married Tres and that within hours of our returning to Texas, he'd apparently left me. I could just ask for his employment records and a copy of his visa without divulging the personal relationship he and I had.

I called Maeve first since she'd already offered to provide employment information, should I need it, but it went to voicemail. When the same happened with my call to Hammer, I figured he was still with Decker, Edge, and Rip.

While all I could focus on presently was my missing husband, I should've pressed harder about his urgent meeting. I was the attorney of record for IISG. Hammer no longer held that position. If anyone should've been included, it was me, not him.

If I allowed my insecurity-driven paranoia to creep in, I could envision a scenario in which they'd rescind the offer of the position, citing my hasty marriage to a man with immigration issues.

Hammer would never throw me under the bus that way, though. We had too much history. If he knew I'd married Tres, he would've approached me in an entirely different way about helping with ICE. He wasn't the type of person to pretend he didn't know something like that. None of the Invincibles were.

While waiting for either Hammer or Maeve to return my call, I circled back to Alejandro. I cringed when the name of the owner of the property on Desert Sunset Drive appeared on the screen and I saw it was the same LLC that owned the house in Austin where Tres lived.

I was so focused on what I was doing, I nearly jumped out of my chair when my phone vibrated seconds later. I slowly turned it over, praying it would be Tres calling. Instead, it was Hammer.

"Hey, Fury," he said when I answered. "I'm sorry I was in such a rush earlier."

"About that. You said you had urgent business to discuss with Decker, Edge, and Rip. I apologize if I'm out of line by asking, but shouldn't I be included in things of that nature if the Invincibles are involved?"

"You should."

"Why wasn't I?"

"What we had to meet about wasn't related to IISG. In fact, it was more of a personal matter—something to do with Rip and Pearl's wedding."

Why the hell had he used the term "urgent business," then?

"As soon as I get the okay to let you in on it, I will."

"Understood. I called about another matter anyway. Could either you or Maeve please forward everything you have in Tres' employee file? Application, visa information, things of that nature."

Hammer didn't respond for several seconds, but I could still make out background noise. I wondered if he'd heard my question and asked it a second time.

"Yeah, Fury, I heard you."

"Is there a problem?"

"Just something I'd rather not admit."

What the hell? Instead of letting my mind race, I counted to ten as I waited for him to continue.

"I'm forwarding the background check we ran on him when we purchased the bar over to you now, but otherwise, there's no file."

"What do you mean?"

"You know Bobby MacIver hired him, right?"

"Makes sense."

"Well, evidently, he wasn't big on record-keeping."

I wasn't surprised, given Bobby was battling cancer. "You're just discovering this now?"

"You know Maeve's history. She didn't think it was that big of a deal. In fact, neither of us paid much attention to the background check until now."

Maeve's family, who were from Ireland, owned one of the most successful chains of pubs in the UK and had for several generations. What she'd look for in a background check would likely be very different from one of the Invincibles.

"You said you didn't pay much attention to the report until today. Does that mean you found something?"

"Affirmative. Tres holds dual citizenships—US and Spanish. His mother is an American expat."

"If he's a US citizen, why was ICE looking for him?"

"That's the million-dollar question, isn't it?"

After ending the call with Hammer, I opened the message he'd forwarded to me. As he'd said, there was nothing out of the ordinary in the file, at least nothing Hammer would've found to be. There was something that rattled me, though. Prior to moving to Texas, Tres' last known address was the Desert Sunset Drive place on the outskirts of Las Vegas, where we'd stayed with Alejandro.

I picked up my cell when it rang, not even bothering to see who was calling. "Storm," I answered out of habit.

"Hey, Fury," said Rebel. "I just talked to Maeve, and she said you had some questions about the ICE guy."

"I do. Did he happen to leave a business card?"

"He didn't, and that's one of the things I wanted to clarify. I feel like a few things got lost in translation. Kind of like that telephone game."

"Can you be more specific?"

"While the guy said he was from ICE, the badge he showed didn't look authentic to me."

"In what way?"

"I know from Edge's badges that they now have holograms or watermarks or whatever you call them. His didn't have one."

"Anything else?"

"My hackles were all the way up. At first, I figured it was just my history with law enforcement. After Edge and I talked about it some more, he suggested maybe it was my instincts tellin' me somethin' was off."

Rebel's husband was not just former MI6. Prior to his service with British intelligence, he had been a highly decorated and respected special forces officer in their military. As one of the founding partners of the Invincibles, his instincts were razor-sharp.

"I wish Edge had been there with me when the man came in. He would've handled it better."

"Who *was* with you, Rebel?"

"We weren't open yet, so it was just Rojo, Bunker, me, and the cleaning crew."

"Do you remember enough about the guy to give a description of him?"

"Sure enough."

"That's great, Rebel. If you or Edge can forward your notes to me, I'd appreciate it."

"You got it, Fury."

"And if you happen to see Tres, would you please ask him to contact me?"

"Sure enough," she repeated before we hung up.

I thought about letting it go to voicemail when a call came in from Vex a few minutes later.

"Hey, Fury, where you at?"

"At home. Why?"

"Scottie and I are on our way to you now."

"Listen, Vex, can this wait? I'm working on this potential immigration issue with Tres right now."

"Is he there?"

"No, but—"

"When's the last time you talked to him?"

"Early this morning. Why?"

"We're less than ten minutes away. We'll fill you in when we get there."

Shit. I hadn't planned to tell anyone Tres was "missing" yet. It appeared I might be forced to.

13

Fury

"What's happening with Kruger?" I asked when Vex and Scottie arrived and I invited them inside.

"The grand jury in Las Vegas is getting ready to hand down indictments on Marco Mancini, Perkins' surviving brother-in-law, along with Stephan Rizzo, Clark County's current sheriff," Scottie answered.

"He's been cleared medically and should arrive here sometime late this afternoon or tomorrow," Vex added.

"Here?"

"He's taking leave," said Vex.

I wouldn't have thought much of his statement if Scottie hadn't opened her mouth like she was about to say something, then immediately shut it.

"Am I missing something?" I asked, looking from her to Vex.

He shrugged. "He may not be returning to the FBI."

I'd run out of patience for pretty much anything when I returned to my house and Tres wasn't there.

Now, my nerves were frayed and my anger management was in full-on failure mode. "Cut to the chase, Vex," I snapped.

"I'd like to add him to the new IISG team."

It dawned on me that I'd be the person drawing up any offer of employment from the Invincibles to Kruger or anyone else. If this was the reason Vex and Scottie had showed up at my house, I'd lose my shit.

"Does this somehow relate to Tres?"

"It doesn't, but—"

"Goddammit, Vex. I asked if whatever it was you wanted to talk to me about could wait. Didn't I?"

"We aren't here to talk about Kruger. You asked about him when we walked in, so I responded. Jesus, Fury, settle down."

Scottie's eyes opened wide at Vex's last two words.

I turned toward her. "Would you excuse us?" I seethed.

"Gladly," she muttered, walking out the front door. I didn't bother watching to see where she went.

"Don't…you…ever…fucking…tell…me…to… settle…down… again. Do you understand me?"

Vex put his hands on his hips. "Maybe that was a poor choice of words, but the woman you just asked to leave found out some very interesting shit about your *husband*, so maybe you do want to *settle the fuck down* enough for her to tell you what it is."

I repeated the tenets of anger management in my head. *Breathe. Progressively relax muscles. Visualize myself calm. Stop and listen.* After taking several deep breaths, relaxing my muscles, beginning with my shoulders, and picturing myself with a smile on my face, I focused on the final of the four.

"Please explain," I said, praying Vex would, rather than provoke me further.

He took a series of deep breaths like I had, stalked over to the front door, and went outside. Seconds later, Scottie came inside, but he didn't.

"Am I the only one who questioned the wisdom behind pairing two people with the code names Fury and Vex?" When she smiled, I did too.

"Did he leave?" I asked.

"No. He's grabbing my computer."

When he stuck his head in the door, I motioned for him to enter.

"Scottie suggested I apologize," muttered Vex.

I heard her sigh and, out of the corner of my eye, saw her shake her head.

"I'm sorry, Fury."

"I am too. I'm pretty tightly wound, but that's no excuse."

Scottie cleared her throat. "Shall we get on with it?"

I motioned for her to take a seat at the table while I filled a pitcher with water and brought it over along with three glasses.

"Before we do, there's something you need to know." I poured myself a glass and took a big swig, wishing it was vodka rather than plain water. "Tres has disappeared."

"Disappeared? What does that mean?" Vex asked.

Knowing only the hard stuff would help at this point, I carried my glass back into the kitchen and opened the freezer, where I kept a bottle of Belvedere. I pulled it out, poured a glass, and downed it before pouring a second and doing the same thing.

"When I returned after the meeting at Hammer's, his stuff was gone. I went by his house, and he's not there either. He's also not answering his phone." I poured a third glass and put the bottle back in the freezer without bothering to offer any to Scottie or Vex. "We haven't spent a single minute apart since we left the Long Branch the night of Rip and Pearl's party."

Rather than look at the two people sitting at my table, I kept my gaze focused out my kitchen window. "Before I left, he agreed to wait for me. Once I returned, we planned to go wedding-ring shopping."

"Well, shit," I heard Vex mumble.

I sat at the table, wishing the two people already seated at it weren't looking at me with such pity.

"After you left, we did some digging," said Scottie, typing something on her keyboard. She turned the screen so I could see it.

Beneath a photo of Tres dressed in a business suit and speaking with three other people, whose backs were to the camera, appeared the caption, "Rare photograph of Leandro Barello III, new CEO of the Santoval Group." The photo that had appeared in *Forbes* was from over a year ago.

"Based on passport records, this was published shortly before Tres arrived in the United States," said Vex.

"What is Santoval Group?"

"According to Fortune Global 500, it ranks eighty-fifth out of all privately held companies in the world. Their headquarters are in Spain, and they operate primarily in the banking sector, but they also have holdings in telecommunications, oil, and gas, as well as construction. Overall, the Santoval Group is valued at close to a hundred billion dollars US."

"What else have you found?"

"Nothing," said Vex.

"Which in itself is perplexing," added Scottie. "That the Barello family is notoriously secretive—to the point of being considered reclusive—explains it in part. There are no known photographs of Tres' father, Leandro Barello Junior, for example, other than a candid photo someone sneaked at his wedding to Tres' mother."

"I don't understand," I said more to myself than to Scottie or Vex. Nothing about this news regarding Tres made sense to me. He was a billionaire CEO of a Fortune 100 company headquartered in Spain, who worked as a bouncer in a bar outside Austin, Texas? I shook my head, got up from the table, sat on the sofa, leaned back, and closed my eyes. "I need to find out if the marriage is valid."

"It is," said Scottie. "I hope you don't think I jumped the gun by checking, but I figured it would be one of the first things you'd want to know."

I opened my eyes and looked over at her. "You're certain?"

"Yes."

Which meant at the ripe old age of thirty, I'd only been married a few hours and would probably be headed to divorce court very soon. What sucked the most was I'd truly believed Tres loved me. I thought we'd spend years and years together. Not days.

"That motherfucker," I said out loud as I hurled a throw pillow, wishing it was something much heavier and that Tres had been on the receiving end rather than an empty wall.

"What do you want to do?" Vex asked.

I wasn't sure where to begin. All I knew for sure was I wanted to be the one to initiate the divorce proceedings before he had the chance to. At least then, I wouldn't be the one "left at the altar" a second time—so to speak. Blake and I hadn't made it that far, and Tres had waited until after we were married to leave me.

I leaned forward and put my head in my hands. As angry as I was, hurt far outweighed it. How could he do this to me? *Why* had he done this to me? I wasn't able to come up with a single scenario that made sense. Besides him being abducted by aliens. Not that that made sense. Even an abduction by non-aliens was illogical. Who would've given him time to pack up his belongings before they kidnapped him?

"Why?" I cried. "Why would he do this?" I said out loud this time, rather than just to myself.

"No clue, Fury," said Vex. Not that I'd expected an answer to my rhetorical question.

I sat up again and wiped my tears. "I need to find him."

"Okay," said Vex. "Where do you want to start?"

The most logical thing would be to inform Hammer and ask for his advice. The idea of doing so nauseated me. However, I doubted I could get much further without him finding out anyway.

"I have no idea."

"What about contacting his family?" Vex asked.

"His reclusive billionaire family? I'm sure that will go well. Can you imagine? 'Hello. I'm Ellison Storm. I need to find your son, who's been slumming it in the States, working as a bouncer in a bar. By the way, we're married. In fact, we just celebrated our forty-eight-hour anniversary. Oh, and the reason I need to find him is so I can serve him with divorce papers.'"

"I know you aren't going to like my next suggestion, but maybe it would be easier if you had another attorney contact the family."

"Lemme guess. Hammer?"

"Again, it would be easier."

I wanted to ask what made him think so. It would be far easier to contact someone I didn't know. Then I wouldn't have to admit how much of an idiot I was.

"Hang on a minute. Before you contact a lawyer, I want to ask you something."

I looked over at Scottie. "What?"

"I was there when you and Tres got married. While I'm no expert, what I saw between you was obviously love. If it hadn't been, I might've questioned why you were being so hasty. But it seemed genuine to me."

"I'm missing the question." I knew I sounded like a bitch, and Scottie didn't deserve the attitude from me. It wasn't her I was mad at. "Sorry," I muttered.

She nodded. "I know I'm overstepping here, but are you sure you want to jump right into divorce proceedings? Why don't you wait until you hear Tres' side of the story?"

Spoken like a woman far more secure than I'd ever been. Or maybe than I had been since Blake Howell trampled on every ounce of self-confidence I'd once possessed. At least where relationships were concerned.

I looked into her eyes and answered as honestly as I could. "Pride."

Scottie nodded. "I get it. I'd probably have the same knee-jerk reaction."

Now, I just wanted to stick my tongue out at her.

She smiled as though she'd guessed what I was thinking. "I suggest we find him first. Then we determine whether divorce is necessary."

I looked from her to Vex. "She would have to be levelheaded."

When he nodded and grinned like a love-sick puppy, my stomach rolled with renewed nausea.

"They live on Mallorca," said Scottie, looking at her computer. "Huge family compound."

"Doesn't Rile DeLéon live on Mallorca?" Vex asked.

"He does." Not only did he live there; Rile's uncle—his father's brother—was the King of Spain. Scottie might be onto something. Out of everyone I knew, Rile would definitely be the most likely to be able to offer advice.

"You need to tell Hammer," said Vex, barely loud enough for me to hear him.

I nodded. It was the last thing I wanted to do, but Vex was right. I needed to tell him. Given he'd said Tres was a "reliable and trusted" employee, I had to fill Maeve and him in on more than just our wedding.

"Fury, I was just about to contact you," he said when he answered my call.

"About?"

"I got a lead on the ICE agent. Actually, I got a lead on the guy who said he was an ICE agent."

"And?"

"Turns out he's a PI."

"How'd you figure that out?"

"Gave Decker the security footage from when the man came into the Branch. It didn't take long for him to get a hit on facial recognition."

I shook my head. Both were things I should've thought of rather than ask Rebel if she could remember what the guy looked like. My head was so far up my butt over Tres that I wasn't thinking straight.

"Scottie was able to dig up some information too. Not on the agent, but on Tres. I'd like to meet with you and Maeve to go over it. There's something else I need to share with you."

"Does this have anything to do with why you turned twelve shades of pale earlier?"

"It does."

"Let's not wait, then. I sense this is something you need to get off your chest."

"Do you already know?"

"I'm not sure how to answer that other than to say I don't operate that way, Fury, and you know it."

"Sorry, Hammer. I do know it."

"Do you mind driving back to the Hammered Dubliner?"

"Not at all. Would it be okay if I asked Scottie and Vex to join us?"

"Sounds like they'd better. Head over now unless there's some reason you can't."

I looked over at Scottie, who nodded.

"See you in about thirty," I said, ending the call and rolling my shoulders. "I, uh, can't drive."

"No, you can't," said Vex, putting his arm around me. "Come on, let's get this over with."

I sat in the backseat of Vex's SUV, trying to clear my head at the same time I rehearsed how I'd tell Hammer and Maeve Tres and I were married. Everything I came up with sounded as stupid as I felt.

"Would you two mind if I called my sister on the way?"

"Of course not," said Scottie. "Do you want us to stop somewhere so you can have some privacy?"

"I'm not going to tell her anything the two of you don't already know."

I was about to end the call after Stephanie's cell rang several times, when I heard her pick up. She sounded out of breath when she said hello.

"Everything okay?" I asked.

"Your niece is working my last nerve."

I smiled. "My niece as opposed to your daughter?"

"I swear I'm about to disown her."

"You'd never do that."

"You're right. Although I might send her to live with you until she turns eighteen. What's up, Ell? You don't sound good."

"Are Mom and Dad still there?"

"Not at the moment. They took the brat and her brother out for ice cream."

As much as I would've preferred the conversation remain focused on whatever was going on between my sister and my niece, I'd called Stephanie for a reason. "There's something I need to tell you."

"Okay." The tone of her voice switched from irritated to concerned. "Out with it."

"Tres and I got married."

If I weren't so heartbroken over his disappearance, I would've laughed when I heard her phone hit the floor.

"Jeez, Ell, you couldn't have warned me to sit down before you told me that?"

"Sorry. I figured it would be better if I didn't beat around the bush, as they say. Before I tell you the next part, I'll warn you to take a seat if you haven't already."

"Are you pregnant?"

Fuck, I hadn't thought of that. I shouldn't be, but wouldn't that just be the icing on the cake?

"Um, no. But—there's no easy way to say this—it appears he may have left town."

"Wait. What? Did you just say it *appears* he did?"

"He's not at my place or his, and I haven't been able to reach him. We'd planned to shop for wedding rings this afternoon."

"Oh my God, Ell, what if he was in an accident? Have you checked local hospitals?"

She made a good point. Once we were finished, I'd ask Scottie to check with both first responders and emergency rooms. I took a deep breath. "There's more."

"More? I'm afraid to ask."

"He's a billionaire. Or his family is. No, he is. Either way, he wasn't honest with me, and now he's gone."

"Shit, Ell. I'm so sorry. Where are you now? Why don't you come over?"

"I'm on my way to a meeting. Plus, I'd rather Mom and Dad don't know about this just yet."

"Understood. I won't say a word."

"Do you swear you won't?"

"I promise, Ell. Not a word. This news should come from you anyway. It isn't my place to tell our parents."

"Thanks, sis."

"What are you going to do?"

"Find the fucking *sonuvabitch*."

Stephanie laughed. "Now you sound more like my sister. Go get him, girl, and if you need help burying him once you find him, you know I'm all in."

It was the same offer she'd made when Blake Howell had ripped my heart to shreds. While I hadn't taken her up on it then, this time, I might just be mad enough to consider it.

14

Fury

"Come on in," said Hammer, greeting us as we approached the front door. "Hold up, Fury," he said after he motioned Vex and Scottie ahead. I should've known he'd call me out when I walked by without making eye contact.

"Before you ask, no, I'm not okay. The sooner we get this over with, the better I'll feel and the more you'll understand."

Rather than respond, Hammer pulled me into a father-like hug. It was the last thing I wanted him to do, given how hard it was for me to keep a rein on my emotions.

"Please, Hammer," I whispered.

He released me and motioned toward the sitting room, where I saw Maeve waiting, holding a bundle of blankets on her lap I assumed was their baby.

"How's she doing?" I whispered.

"She's perfect," she said, moving the blanket so I could see the sleeping little girl.

I took a seat on the opposite sofa so Hammer could sit next to his wife. When the four others in the room looked at me, I folded my hands and squared my shoulders.

"Tres and I were married when we were in Las Vegas," I blurted.

While Maeve's eyes opened wide, Hammer had more practice masking his reaction.

"Congratulations," he said, then waited for me to continue.

"After I left our meeting this morning, I went home, where I expected him to be waiting. He was gone, as were his belongings. I haven't been able to reach him since."

Maeve's expression didn't change as she looked from me to her husband, then back again.

"I also went by his place, and he wasn't there. Neither was his car. Scottie checked with first responders and hospitals; however, there were no reports of accidents with injuries this morning either within Austin city limits or on the outskirts."

Hammer took it all in the same way he would in a briefing.

I turned to Scottie. "Could you take it from here?"

She nodded. "I did some digging into Tres' background." Like she'd done earlier, she set her laptop on the coffee table between the two sofas and turned it so Hammer and Maeve could see the screen.

"What in the bloody hell?" Maeve muttered. Her eyes met mine. "Is this real?"

"It appears to be."

"Tres is Leandro Barello's son?"

"Do you know him?" I asked her.

"I know of him. Very few actually know the man."

"Apparently, the same can be said for his son," I muttered.

"Fascinating," she added, leaning back against the sofa.

Hammer's reaction was less obvious, but I knew him well enough to predict he was more angry than stunned. He sat back like Maeve had, but folded his arms. "This explains the PI."

"Do you think it has something to do with his disappearance?" Maeve asked.

"It's a clue," he responded.

"Given the family's reclusivity, it seems unlikely I'd have much luck contacting Tres' parents."

"Certainly not," agreed Maeve.

"Vex had an idea, though. The Barellos have a compound on Mallorca. We thought Rile might have an in or at least a way to get in touch with the family."

Hammer nodded. "I was thinking the same thing." He sat forward and rested his elbows on his knees, then looked directly at me. "Given the timing of the PI showing up, the fact that Tres has not been in touch with either Maeve or me, and you haven't been able to reach him, I'm going to suggest we treat this as though he was taken against his will."

"Good of his kidnappers to pack up his belongings when they abducted him."

Hammer raised a brow. "It made you assume he just left, didn't it?"

"Good point," added Maeve.

I had to concede it was, not that I'd admit it out loud.

Hammer checked his watch. "It's almost midnight in Spain. While Rile may be a night owl, I'm not sure Kensington is."

"Especially now," said Maeve, turning to me. "I speak from experience. Rile recently mentioned Kensington is pregnant."

"Maybe I shouldn't bother them with this."

Hammer shook his head. "I wouldn't look at it that way." He took a deep breath and let it out slowly. "As I said before, my gut is telling me we should act on the supposition that Tres' disappearance was not his own doing."

The idea the man I loved had been kidnapped was far harder to deal with than the notion he merely decided he didn't want to be with me. When I turned my head away as my eyes filled with tears, Scottie squeezed my hand.

Hammer took out his phone and typed something on the screen, then looked up at me. "It's your call who knows you're married. I've alerted both Decker and Rile that we believe Tres may be missing, although to Rile, I said it was a member of our staff. I'm sure Ashford will respond first." Before he finished his sentence, his cell vibrated. "I stand corrected. Rile beat him to it."

"It's easier if they know," I said.

"Agreed." Hammer tapped his screen and brought the phone to his ear. "Thanks for your quick response. There's a situation I want to make you aware of and ask for your guidance."

After getting Rile's permission to put the call on speaker and identifying those in the room, we took turns briefing him in the same way we had Hammer and Maeve.

"Knowing as much as I do about the Barello family as well as the Santoval Group, I am as stunned as I'm sure you are to hear Tres was living in Texas and working at the Long Branch. Please understand I mean no offense, but are you certain it was him?" Rile asked.

"As certain as we can be. Unless he has a twin with the same name," Hammer responded.

"I will need to give this some thought. You are correct to suggest getting in touch with Leandro Barello regarding the whereabouts of his son will not be easy. And by that, I mean both him being in Texas for the last several months as well as his alleged disappearance."

Hammer thanked him before ending the call.

"According to the background check you forwarded to me, the only prior address listed for Tres was the place in Las Vegas where he and I stayed with a friend of his. At the very least, I'd like to check with Alejandro, the man we stayed with, to see if he's heard from him or knows where he might be."

Hammer nodded in agreement.

"However, I don't know how to get in touch with him."

"Do you want Decker to run a check on the property and see if he can find a way to reach this guy?"

"I already did. The deed is held by an LLC, *Activos Comerciales de Mallorca*, which translates to Business Assets of Mallorca. As far as contact information, the only thing listed is a post office box. Oh, and the same LLC owns Tres' place in Austin."

"While we wait to hear from Rile, why don't you return to Vegas and see what you can find out from this friend?"

"Roger that," I said, standing to leave.

"Vex, you go with her," Hammer added. "Scottie, maybe you should too."

"Roger that," Vex said like I had. Scottie nodded her agreement.

"Lemme see about the plane." Hammer tapped the screen of his cell and waited. "Yeah, it's still here," he said a couple of minutes later. "Head out, and I'll follow up with Decker about a departure time."

After leaving the ranch, Vex and Scottie dropped me off at my house and said they'd pick me up once we received word from Hammer to proceed to the airfield.

I dreaded walking inside alone. Earlier, I'd been anxious to crawl back in bed with my husband. It hurt like hell, knowing Tres wasn't under the covers, waiting for me. As much as I'd pushed him away in the few days after we spent our first night together, now I hated not being with him.

Instead of packing like I knew I should, I lay on the bed and rested my head on the pillow he'd used hours ago. As I breathed in his lingering scent, my tears turned into sobs. How dare the universe rip love out of my hands so soon after I'd finally been willing to accept it?

"Come for me, *mi tormenta*." I woke with a start, bolting upright when I could swear I heard Tres' voice.

I got out of bed and went into the kitchen. "Where are you, Tres?" I said aloud. "Help me find you."

I leaned against the counter, tears running down my cheeks as I cursed the silence.

The flight from Austin to Las Vegas was another painful reminder of the happiness I'd felt with Tres the last time we were on this plane. Then, we'd been planning our honeymoon. I rested my head against my seat, closed my eyes, and thought about the man I'd married.

Nothing about him added up, and it began long before I'd met him. Why had he been living in Texas, working as a bouncer in the first place? Why hadn't the fact he was a billionaire from Spain shown up on the background check Hammer ran on him?

On one hand, all the evidence appeared to support the theory that Leandro Barello III wasn't at all the man either Hammer or I believed him to be.

On the other hand, I trusted Hammer's instincts, and if his gut was telling him Tres hadn't just skipped town, it was worth paying attention to.

I groaned. Then again, Hammer hadn't known the man was a billionaire, either.

I opened my eyes and saw Vex studying me. When he stood and walked toward the plane's aft, I followed.

"What are you thinking?" he asked.

"About?"

"You tell me."

"What else? Tres."

"And?"

I reiterated everything I'd been thinking out loud to him, including the fact Hammer hadn't known Tres as well as he thought he did.

"Let me ask you this. How would you feel if you found out Tres traveled somewhere, didn't tell you, but he's fine? Meaning, not in any kind of danger."

"I'd be pissed."

"What else?" Vex pressed.

"You know the answer, or you wouldn't be asking."

"Tell me anyway."

"Relieved but pissed. Really pissed."

"Would you rather he be a jerk or a victim of kidnapping?"

"Now you're being a jerk."

Vex smiled. "But you know I'm right."

"Right? I'm not sure what about. While you may believe you proved a point, there's no one I would want to be a kidnapping victim over a jerk."

"Scottie wasn't the only one at your wedding who knew you and Tres loved each other. Sorry, I didn't mean to use past tense. *Do* love each other."

I sat in an empty seat near where we were standing. "More than anything, I just want to find him. I want to know he's safe, and I want to understand why he wasn't forthright about his background or his family. I want to know why he was working in a bar in Texas if his 'day job' was CEO of a company worth billions."

Rather than hire a car service, Vex, Scottie, and I rented a vehicle once we landed at the Las Vegas airport. I was more than happy to let Vex drive while I navigated.

Once we reached the development, Scottie used her FBI credentials to get us through the guarded gate.

"Wow," Vex muttered when we pulled up to the house on Desert Sunset Drive.

"I said the same thing when I first saw it."

He cut the engine, and we got out of the car. After a moment of hesitation, I approached the front door while he and Scottie stayed a few feet back. I pressed the intercom, waited a few seconds, then pressed it again. There was no response either time.

"Where's Vex?" I asked Scottie when I turned around and saw he was gone.

"He went around back to take a look." She pointed to the southern side of the house.

I stood with my hands on my hips. "I guess we can wait and see if anyone shows up."

"This is either the most minimalistic interior design I've ever seen, or this house is empty," said Vex, coming around from the side opposite of where Scottie had pointed.

"What do you mean?"

Vex motioned and I followed.

"I'll wait in the car," Scottie shouted after us.

"Does she think we're going to break in or something?"

Vex shook his head. "Since she's still an official agent with the Federal Bureau of Investigation, I'm sure she'd rather not speculate."

"Right."

I peeked in the first window we came to. All the furniture that had been in the place a day ago was gone. "You're right. It's empty."

"It was the same with every window I looked in."

"What the fuck?" I said under my breath.

"Ditto," muttered Vex.

15

Fury

Hammer repeated the same words Vex and I had said when I called to tell him the house was empty.

"I don't have any other ideas about how to find the man Tres and I stayed with."

"You might as well come home. I don't expect to hear from Rile between now and when you land. Once I have, we'll figure out the next steps."

"Come straight here," Hammer said when I called him four hours later to say we'd arrived at the Austin airfield.

"What's going on?"

"We'll talk more when you get here."

The air left my lungs, and I gripped Vex's arm to steady myself. "Have you found Tres?"

"No, we haven't, and I'm sorry, sweetheart. I spoke with Rile about an hour ago. As I said, we'll go over it once you're here."

Shortly after we walked in, Hammer initiated a video conference with Rile.

"It is nice to see you, Fury," he said when I sat down at the table where Hammer had set the laptop. "As it so often seems, I wish it were under better circumstances."

"I wish it were too."

"You should be aware that while I do not know the family well, those I've spoken with who do, had many good things to say about Tres."

"Thank you for passing that on, Rile."

"Which makes me agree with Hammer regarding his disappearance. I'm sorry to say I fear foul play."

My heart sank. I feared the same, but hearing him say it, made it feel worse.

"Perhaps we could speak alone for a few minutes," said Rile.

I looked over at Hammer.

"Of course," he said before leading Vex and Scottie out of the room.

"Go ahead," I told Rile once the door closed behind them.

"The Barello family's estate is on the opposite side of the Bay of Palma from mine and is three times the size."

"Have you visited?"

"Only once, with my uncle."

"The king?"

Rile smiled and nodded. "It was many years ago, and I remember little besides its grandeur."

"You mentioned you spoke with people who know Tres?"

"Yes, shared business associates spoke highly of him. However, there were rumors he did not accept the position of CEO willingly."

"Why not?"

"I am not certain. However, his father is said to be quite imposing. Again, a rumor since he has been out of the public eye most of his life."

"What about Tres' mother?"

"Amanda is also a very private woman. She is the patron of many foundations both here on Mallorca and in all of Spain. Like the Barellos, the Fernandez-Yerena family is quite wealthy. When Amanda and Leandro married, the festivities were said to be on par with the most lavish royal weddings. As you know, she is American."

"Does Tres have siblings?"

"Sadly, no. However, Leandro has a younger brother, who has sired several nieces and nephews."

"Several?"

"Seven in total."

I couldn't help but wonder if Tres was close to any of his cousins. If we were unable to speak with his parents directly, perhaps one of them would know why he'd traveled first to Nevada, then to Texas. Something else dawned on me. "Do you happen to know if one is named Alejandro?"

Rile's eyes scrunched. "I do not. Why do you ask?"

"We stayed with someone by that name when we were in Las Vegas. He was introduced by his first name only and as a friend. At one point, though, Tres referred to him as his 'most trusted associate.'"

"I will attempt to find out if Tres has close allies within Santoval with that name."

"Allies?" It seemed a surprising choice of words.

"Family businesses of that magnitude often operate with opposing sides."

"Are you suggesting someone in Tres' family may be responsible for his disappearance?"

"If we were to discover they were, it would not come as a surprise."

"What else do you know about the family business?" I asked.

"It is rumored at least one of Leandro's nephews is quite active in the management of Santoval assets."

"If that's the case and Tres didn't want it, why wasn't he offered the CEO position?"

"Quite simply because the nephew is the son of the *second* son, not the first."

My eyes scrunched. "Seriously? What would've happened if, instead of a boy, Leandro and his wife had a girl?"

"I can only speculate that having additional children would've become a more urgent matter."

"The eldest daughter would not have been thrust into the position of CEO unwillingly?"

"It would not have been permitted. The Barello family is eccentric," he seemed to add as an afterthought.

I was stunned. "That isn't eccentric, Rile. It's misogynistic. Not to mention antiquated. If Tres had no interest in the role and one of his cousins did, it should've been given to them."

"Please understand I am stating the facts as I believe them to be, not endorsing the methodology."

"I'm sorry. I didn't mean to suggest you were."

Rile bowed his head as if to say he accepted my apology before continuing. "Hammer and I have been discussing the next course of action and think it may be best for you to come to Mallorca."

"Do you think Tres is there?"

"Maybe, and if not yet, there is a chance he's on his way. However, not necessarily of his own accord. I also believe I may be able to arrange for you to meet with his parents."

"I mean no disrespect, Rile, but to what end?"

"The stated purpose would be that you are in Mallorca as the legal representative of a firm in which Tres has an interest."

"Then what?"

"First, we will ascertain whether either Leandro or Amanda know their son's whereabouts."

"After that?"

"What we do next will depend on what we learn from our first objective."

"And you believe I should be there?"

Rile nodded slowly. "I do."

"Then, I'll come."

"Very good."

After he said he'd be back in touch once he'd made the necessary travel arrangements, we ended the video conference and I went in search of Hammer, Vex, and Scottie.

"Rile wants me to come to Mallorca," I blurted when I found them in the sitting room.

Hammer nodded. "He and I discussed it, and I agree. I'm going to make another suggestion."

My eyes met his. "Go ahead."

"I don't want you traveling to Mallorca alone."

"Hammer, I—"

"We've already talked about it," interrupted Vex. "Scottie and I will go with you."

"And?" Hammer appeared to be prompting him.

"Kruger will be traveling with us."

"Is it really necessary?" I asked.

"If this turns into a rescue mission, I want you to have the resources necessary to mount an op without delay," Hammer responded.

I put my hand on my stomach when it lurched. "Understood."

"You'll get departure information directly from Decker, but I suggest you be prepared to leave very soon. And, Fury, while you're in the air, see if you can draft and execute an employment agreement with Kruger."

"Roger that," I responded.

A few minutes later, I received a text from Decker, saying our flight would leave out of the same airfield in Austin we'd just come from. We'd travel first to New York, where we'd need to refuel before crossing the Atlantic. Flight time was projected at four hours. It would be another eight before we landed at the airport on the island of Mallorca.

I also received confirmation from Rile that he'd have a car waiting and a driver would bring us from there to his compound, where we'd be staying.

Once in the air, I drafted an employment agreement between IISG and Kruger Dunning, as Hammer had requested.

"Is this amount right?" Kruger asked when I gave it to him to read over. Having had a similar reaction when I saw the amount of my retainer, I assured him it was correct.

"Damn, I should've left the FBI years ago."

"They wouldn't have made you this offer years ago," I teased.

"I have another question."

"Go ahead."

"Who is in my chain of command?"

"That will be mission-dependent." I anticipated his next question, so I went ahead and answered. "For this one, it will be Vex."

Kruger nodded and continued his review of the document. Vex was seated on the opposite side of the plane, and when I looked over at him, he rolled his eyes.

I hadn't noticed when we were in Las Vegas, but Kruger looked enough like his brother that if one didn't already know they weren't the same age, they might think the two men were twins.

Both were handsome, with sandy-blond hair and piercing green eyes. However, neither was my type. While I hadn't realized it until recently, my ideal man was a tall Spanish guy with eyes the color of my favorite bourbon, hair as brown as my own, a body that brought me pleasure like I'd never known, and a voice that seemed to speak directly to my soul.

I had to find him, and when I did, I'd make him promise, like he had that first night, not to leave me again.

16

Fury

When we landed in Mallorca the following day, it was sunny but cool, similar to the weather in Texas in early February. Knowing evening temperatures could dip below freezing, I had packed appropriate clothes and was grateful I'd decided to wear a sweater on the plane.

As promised, an SUV was waiting for us on the tarmac when we deplaned. I had only been to Mallorca once before, for Rile and Kensington's wedding. It had been a quick trip, and I hadn't seen much of the rest of the island. However, taking in the views now, it was easy to understand why Rile had made it his home.

The man himself was waiting for us when we pulled into the compound and up to the main house.

"Welcome to my home," he said, greeting me first, then the others. "My apologies for Kensington not being here. She is not feeling well and went to lie down."

"Maeve mentioned you're pregnant."

Rile beamed. "It is true."

"Congratulations."

"Many thanks." He motioned in the direction of the bay. "While Pedro shows the others to their accommodations, please take a walk with me, Fury."

I followed him across a courtyard and over to a path I knew led down to the beach. Rile stood beside me and pointed to the other side of the bay.

"Do you see the sunlight's reflection?" he asked.

"Yes."

"That is the Barello compound."

Even from a distance, it appeared imposing, the same word Rile had used when he spoke of Tres' father.

We stood in silence, looking out across the water, then suddenly, Rile's face broke into a wide smile. He abruptly turned, looked up, and waved. When I turned too, I saw Kensington standing on a balcony, waving back.

"You knew she was there before you turned around, didn't you?"

He grinned. "Of course."

Like the rumors Rile had mentioned he'd heard about the Barello family, I had been privy to a few about him. Mainly that he was believed to have a sixth sense. "How?"

"When your true love is near, you will feel their presence long before you see them, my friend."

While the sentiment was sweet, witnessing Rile's love for his wife was a painful reminder that I had no idea where in the world my own love might be, and once we found him, if I would discover everything he'd made me believe had been a lie.

"I have requested a meeting with Leandro and Amanda Barello but have yet to receive a confirmation of when and where it might take place."

"But you believe it will?"

His Cheshire Cat grin returned. "It would be impossible for them to refuse the audience, given the request came from their king."

"Thank you, Rile."

He patted my hand. "It is what we do, Fury, as you are aware."

"I doubt asking favors from royalty is something we do very often."

"Only when necessary."

It was common knowledge within IISG that Rile had connections not just to the king and queen of Spain on his father's side of the family, but also to the Queen of England on his mother's side. It was how he'd met

Kensington, who was the Queen's grandniece on the consort's side of the family.

"I will allow you to get settled now." Rile glanced over his shoulder and smiled. I didn't need to look to know his wife was still in view.

As if summoned telepathically, Pedro appeared in a golf cart.

"I don't remember seeing these hillside cottages when I was here before," I said when he parked in front of one.

"These four have recently been renovated," Pedro explained in an accent more British than Spanish when I asked about them. "Your bags were delivered to the Whitby cottage, ma'am." I smiled, remembering Whitby was Kensington's maiden name. If only everyone could experience a love like Rile and his wife shared, what a different world it might be.

"Welcome," said Kensington, greeting Vex, Scottie, Kruger, and me when we arrived at the main house later for dinner.

"Thank you so much, and I hope we're not too much of an intrusion," I said as we cheek-kissed.

"Never. I enjoy the company, and it is so good to see you again."

"How are you feeling?" I leaned closer and asked.

"Far better at the end of the day than I do at the beginning. However, I will not complain, given the reason."

Marta, who lived with Rile and Kensington in the main house and had been his cook and housekeeper for years, had prepared a feast of traditional Spanish cuisine. And while his wife didn't partake in any wine, Rile continued to pour some of the best Rioja I'd ever tasted.

"Are you aware I am on the board of the Barello family's AMALEAN charity?" Kensington asked partway through our meal. "We currently have forty homes on the island for families who are impoverished or mothers and children who have experienced domestic violence. We hope to double the number by the year's end."

"Do you know them very well?" I asked.

Kensington looked at her husband, and they both smiled. "While I have communicated with Amanda Barello, I've yet to meet the woman in person."

"She is as reclusive as her husband," I commented.

"I fear so."

I heard a cell phone ring.

"Excuse me. I would not take a call during dinner; however, I believe it's news of our requested meeting." Rile stood, picked up his mobile, and left the room.

"As much as I would like to go along, I think it best if the two of you go alone," said Kensington.

"Rile and me?" I asked.

She nodded and looked up at him when her husband returned.

"We have been invited for dinner tomorrow evening," he announced.

"We?" I asked.

"You, Kensington, and myself," he confirmed, offering his apologies to Vex, Scottie, and Kruger.

None of the three appeared disappointed, given Rile had spent much of dinner talking about the family's eccentricities.

"My goodness," Kensington said under her breath. "I don't suppose it would do to beg off this invitation. Not that I'd want to."

Rile rested his hand on her shoulder. "If you aren't feeling up to it, you are not required to go with us, my love."

"While I tend to be tired later in the day, it is better than the nausea I experience in the morning. I certainly wouldn't have been able to accept if they'd invited us for breakfast. Not that they would have."

Presently, I was the nauseated one. Tomorrow evening, I would meet Tres' parents. Not that meeting them necessarily meant I'd be any closer to knowing where he was.

By midafternoon the following day, I was miserable. Or maybe it was the people around me who were, since I was grouchy to the point Vex pulled me aside and told me to chill the fuck out—not his exact words but close enough.

I could not remember a single time in my life when I was as nervous as I felt now. No matter how many deep breaths I took, muscle relaxation, or visualization techniques I tried, nothing made a dent in my anxiety.

"Come," said Rile, motioning me over to the trail that led to the beach. We walked down the pathway almost to the sand. I took a seat on a boulder when he did the same.

"I sense your unease," he began.

"Rile, you wouldn't need to be clairvoyant in order to."

He looked out at the ocean. "At a very young age, I learned royalty, celebrities, professional athletes, and the like are regular mortals just as we are. There is no need to be anxious in their presence. They are no different than you or me."

"What about in-laws? Are you telling me there's no reason to be anxious around them? Not that they'll know I'm their daughter-in-law."

Rile shrugged and chuckled. "Neither of Kensington's parents played an active role in her life. In the little time we've spent with them, they behaved more like the children and Kenzie and I the parents. Thus, I cannot empathize."

Somehow, I doubted the same would be true for the Barellos.

Within five minutes of our arrival, it was clear to me that Tres' father was every bit the misogynistic asshole I'd expected him to be, based on what Rile had said about the Santoval Group. I still had trouble believing an eldest daughter wouldn't have been permitted to be CEO.

Tres' mother, on the other hand, was gracious and welcoming, eager to speak with Kensington and me on our own.

Amanda, as she insisted I call her, poured a glass of wine for me and water for Kensington when she declined the offer. When she patted her stomach by way of an explanation, Tres' mother nodded knowingly.

"Mr. DeLéon tells me you're part of the legal team for one of his companies," she said, leading us out to a solarium.

"She is actually the solicitor of record for several of his entities," clarified Kensington. Not that it was entirely truthful.

"Well done, then," our hostess said, motioning for us to take a seat.

"I'm here on behalf of one of his holdings," I began in the way Rile and I had decided to be the best approach. "Regarding your son."

Amanda raised a brow and immediately looked inside, appearing to relax once she determined her husband was far enough away he hadn't heard me. "What about him?" she asked in a voice barely above a whisper.

"As I'm sure you're aware, Tres was in the States, working for a man who is a partner in one of Mr. DeLéon's businesses."

The woman's eyes darted between mine and the view of her husband. "Go on."

I kept my voice low. "Mr. Anderson, Tres' employer, grew concerned when he was unable to reach him earlier in the week after he neglected to show up for an important meeting. Have you been in recent contact with your son?"

The woman paled. I glanced at her hands folded on her lap and noticed her grip was tight.

"I have not spoken with him recently," she finally responded.

"Could you perhaps try reaching him, either now or after dinner?" Kensington asked.

The tension seeping from Tres' mother seemed to increase, and her eyes continued to dart from us to where her husband stood, speaking with Rile.

Something was up. Either Amanda knew where Tres was and didn't want us to know, or she was attempting to hide her concern enough that her husband wouldn't pick up on it.

"Mrs. Barello?"

"After dinner," she said in a clipped voice. "We should join the gentlemen now." When she stood and left the room, Kensington and I followed.

There was no further mention of Tres during dinner, given his father continued to lead all conversations around to Rile's uncle and aunt.

"Do the king and queen have plans to visit Mallorca in the near future?" he asked.

"I believe they do," Rile responded. The answer appeared to please Mr. Barello.

"We should make it a point to visit with them when they are here."

A quick glance in Kensington's and Amanda's direction confirmed both women appeared stunned but masked their reactions just as fast.

As part of our plan had not included asking Tres' father about his son unless Amanda did, following my questions to her about him, there wasn't any mention of him until close to the end of dinner.

"I heard a rumor your son took over as CEO of the Santoval Group," said Rile. "I hope the news means you intend to enjoy some time away from the daily grind businesses are sometimes plagued by."

"Yes," Leandro responded but, otherwise, said nothing else about his son.

I surreptitiously studied the man. Like with Amanda, something was up. I sensed they knew more about Tres' disappearance than either was willing to say.

Once we were finished with the final course of the evening's meal, Tres' mother offered to give us a tour of their palatial-looking home. I'd expected it would be limited to the areas on the main level and was surprised when she led us up a grand staircase.

She pointed to paintings hung in the hallway we walked down, identifying some of her husband's ancestors, but not all.

We reached a door at the end, and I noticed her hand shook as she grasped the knob and opened it. She led us into a suite larger than the one Tres and I had stayed in when we were in Las Vegas.

"This used to be my son's room," she said unnecessarily, given there were signs of him everywhere I looked. After Kensington excused herself to the lavatory, I walked around the room, studying photos of Tres as a boy and teenager.

Amanda walked over and shut the door Rile's wife had left ajar. "I know who you are," she said.

I turned in her direction but didn't speak.

"Until very recently, my son and I spoke daily. While I knew he was in the States, my husband did not. He is also unaware of your marriage."

"I see."

"Tres and his father had a falling out and are estranged. A state they have been in for much of our son's adult life."

"Is that why he was in Texas?"

"I'm not certain why he chose that particular area. However, I do know he did his best to keep his whereabouts from his dad." She walked over to a window and looked out. I joined her.

"Mr. DeLéon—Cortez—mentioned your son accepted the position of CEO unwillingly."

"That is one way of putting it."

"How would you put it?" I asked.

"He wanted no part of the family business. Out of respect for my husband and me, he kept his feelings known only to us. At least, that's what I believed until you said Cortez was aware Tres didn't want the position."

"Mrs. Barello—Amanda—while I don't wish to alarm you, we believe Tres' disappearance may not have been of his own choosing."

"I have reason to believe you're correct in that assessment." She turned her back to the view and sat on a cushioned window seat. When she patted it, I sat beside her. "My son loves you, Ms. Storm, or should I say Mrs. Barello?"

My breath caught, and my eyes filled with unexpected tears. It was such a relief to know I hadn't been wrong about Tres. More, that he'd told his mother about me and that we'd married. However, that she believed there was more to his disappearance than keeping his father from knowing where he was, added to my worry.

"I love him too," I said, wiping at a tear that rolled down my cheek.

"I believe you do."

"I am also very worried about him."

"As am I, which is why I pushed my husband to agree to tonight's dinner."

"You said you have reason to believe my theory about your son's disappearance is correct. May I ask why?"

"Mainly due to the fact I haven't heard from him. It is completely unlike Tres. He would not allow me to worry about him intentionally. Also, in our last conversation, Tres said he planned to tell you about his family and the life in Spain he left behind. He also told me he planned to bring you to Mallorca."

I could no longer keep a rein on my emotions, and my tears flowed freely. "I don't understand why he didn't tell me before we married."

"At first, it was a matter of concealing his identity to everyone. He worked very hard to maintain his anonymity."

"If that were the case, why didn't he use an alias?"

"I suppose because, regardless of his relationship with his father, Tres was proud of who he was, proud of his heritage, proud of his family. I don't believe he intended to stay away as long as he did. Shortly before he told me about you, he mentioned he planned to return to Mallorca to confront his father and make it known he would not serve as CEO of Santoval now or in the future."

We both abruptly stood when we heard footsteps in the hallway and breathed the same sigh of relief when Kensington walked into the room.

"My husband sent a message saying Leandro is wondering where we'd run off to."

"We should rejoin them." Amanda turned to me and took one of my hands in hers. "I will make arrangements for us to meet in the morning so we can continue our conversation."

I nodded and followed both women to where Rile and Tres' father waited. We left a short while later, after Kensington apologized and said she was feeling quite tired.

"Tres' mother knows about me and that he and I are married," I blurted once we were in the car and had driven out the gates of the Barello compound.

The look on Rile's face did not mirror the stunned expression on Kensington's.

"I take it his father doesn't know," she commented.

"Correct."

"Which is why she said she'd make arrangements for you to meet in the morning before we left Tres' room."

"Yes. She also believes Tres is in danger, or at least that his disappearance wasn't of his own doing." I filled them in on the rest of what Amanda and I had talked about, including Tres' intention to come clean about his background as well as bringing me to Mallorca.

"It makes my heart happy to know he told her about you," said Kensington, looking over the seat at me.

While it made mine happy too, my worry over him was increasing by the minute. My eyes met Rile's in the rearview mirror.

"What are you thinking?" I asked.

"If Tres has, in fact, been kidnapped, I would expect a ransom demand should be issued soon."

I agreed. If one wasn't, it would indicate his disappearance had nothing to do with money. I couldn't allow myself to think what that would mean.

I received a message from Amanda Barello not long after we'd returned to Rile's compound, saying she would make arrangements to visit with us here in the morning. I passed the news on to Rile before he dropped me off at the guesthouse. Given there were four, I was staying alone in one and appreciated the time on my own.

After making myself a cup of chamomile tea and changing into the T-shirt I slept in, I sat by the window and looked out at the view of the moonlight on the water.

I was terribly worried about Tres, and at the same time, filled with a sense of peace about our relationship. My heart felt so full, knowing he'd told his mother about me and that he'd planned to bring me here to meet his family.

After checking the time and realizing it was midafternoon in Texas, I called my sister. She answered on the first ring.

"Any news?" she asked.

"I haven't found Tres yet, but I did meet his parents."

Stephanie gasped. "His billionaire parents?"

"Yes, and they are every bit as haughty as you'd expect. His father more than his mother."

"Does this mean you're in Spain?"

When I worked for the CIA, my family had learned not to ask where I was, where I was headed, or when I'd be back. I'd become more relaxed about it after I left the agency and returned to school to get my law degree, then went to work for the Invincibles. However, sometimes, secrecy was necessary in my role with them as well. "I am. Mallorca, in fact."

"I've always wanted to travel to Spain. I bet it's so beautiful."

"It really is, sis. I hope, one day soon, you'll be able to see it."

"Just so you know, I've kept your secret. I didn't even tell Jimmy."

I silently prayed that within the next few days, I could tell my parents Tres and I were married. First, I had to find him. Before I could move forward with anything in my life, I had to find him.

17

Fury

While I had no idea what I'd expected prior to Amanda Barello's arrival at Rile and Kensington's home, it certainly wasn't the way she showed up.

Shortly after ten in the morning, Vex, Scottie, Kruger, and I were sitting in the kitchen, having an informal breakfast with our hosts, when Rile received an alert on his phone that someone had arrived at the front gate. He pulled up the security feed and held his mobile so I could see the screen. Behind the wheel of a modest silver compact car sat a woman I knew was Tres' mother despite the oversized hat and sunglasses she wore. Rile tapped the screen, and the gate opened, allowing her entry.

He and I got up from the table and walked outside to greet her.

"Good morning," I said, walking over to the car when she got out. Amanda removed her hat and glasses, tossed them on the car seat, then held her hand out to me. When I took it, she pulled me into an unexpected and tight embrace.

"Now you're here, we will find my son together," she said, brushing a tear from her cheek.

We led her inside, where I introduced her to the three people who had traveled with me and who I explained would help us find Tres. Before taking a seat, I offered her coffee or tea and Kensington invited her to join us for breakfast. The woman surprised me again with her relaxed ways when she chose coffee and fixed herself a plate from the food that had been served family style.

Once I'd taken a seat, Rile started out by assuring Amanda the people Tres worked for in the US were already searching for her son there, while others were initiating the same in Europe. He then asked if she'd mind if he took notes on his laptop while we talked. She said it was fine for him to do so.

"Do you have any theories as to where your son might be?" he began.

"Until I learned of his relationship with Ellison, I could not have ventured a guess. However, regardless of where in the world he was, I would have heard from him within a day or two. Given I have not, I can say with absolute certainty, wherever he is, it is against his will."

"Neither you nor your husband have received a ransom demand, is that correct?" Rile asked next.

"We have not. If Leandro had, it is not something he would have kept from me."

"Can you think of anyone who might have a motive to kidnap your son?" I asked.

"The most obvious would be my husband's brother, Baltasar."

"Because it would clear the way for his son to take over as CEO of Santoval?" I asked.

"Not exactly." Amanda rested against her chair and sighed. "While I love my husband very much, I have never agreed with the way his family's business is structured. There is no way for anyone besides the eldest son of the eldest son to take over as the head of the company." She sighed a second time. "Even when the son has no interest in doing so."

"Is that what happened with Tres?"

She rested her hand on mine and squeezed my fingers. "From the time he was a small boy, he expressed no desire to follow in his father's footsteps. The older he got, the wider the gap between the two became."

"Why did your husband step down?" Riled asked.

"His doctors warned him if he kept working the way he was, he would be dead within the year from either a massive heart attack or a stroke. He'd already suffered one heart episode and had done nothing to change his lifestyle in the way the team of cardiologists told him he must. If it weren't for his father's health issues, Tres never would've agreed to be named interim CEO. It was his understanding at the time that was all it would be. He fully expected his father would return to the position within a few months at most."

"What changed?"

"Are you asking why Tres left?" She answered my question with her own.

"I am."

"Tres came by the house, as he did most every day, to review reports with his father. While I was not in the room at the time, I could hear raised voices. I opened the door to my husband's study at the same time Tres accused his father of lying to him. Leandro insisted he'd never said he had any intention of returning as CEO and demanded Tres continue to do his duty to his family and the company. The accusations and harsh words continued with Tres saying his father had manipulated him. Then he told his father he quit. Leandro made everything worse by responding that he could never quit. It was his destiny to take over, and he had no choice but to remain as CEO until such time as he had a son of his own old enough to run Santoval."

"Is that when he left?"

Amanda hung her head and nodded. "He swore he would never speak to his father again, and Leandro threatened to cut him off and disinherit him. Tres responded that if he were really to do it, it would be the happiest day of his life."

"Who has been running Santoval since Tres left? Alejandro?" It was a hunch, and I had no idea if I'd guessed correctly that the man I met in Las Vegas was her nephew.

I knew I had when Amanda's eyes opened wide. "Alejandro? Never. He and Tres were in agreement that the way the company was passed down from generation to generation should change. Not that the board would've gone along with it unless Leandro initiated the motion. Either way, when Tres left, Alejandro did as well."

"Do you know his whereabouts?"

"I do not."

"What about how to get in touch with him?" I asked.

"I have been trying but to no avail."

"Would Baltasar know how to reach him?"

Amanda shook her head. "The two are estranged in the same way Leandro and Tres are."

"Cortez mentioned Alejandro has several siblings. Would it be possible to reach out to any of them regarding their brother's whereabouts?"

"Perhaps."

"Who stepped in after Tres and Alejandro left Santoval?"

"Baltasar's second son, Pascual."

"Is he CEO now?"

Tres' mother shook her head. "No. He isn't even on the board, nor is his father. While Pascual may be acting as interim CEO, he would *never* be given the title."

"Could he sabotage the company in any way?" I asked.

Amanda shook her head again. "His power is limited by the board of directors."

I hated to bring up the next question. Just saying the words nearly broke my heart. "What if Tres passed away?"

She took a deep breath and let it out slowly. "If Leandro was unable to return as CEO, the board would have no choice but to appoint the next in line—Baltasar."

"He certainly has a motive, then," said Vex, who until now had remained silent in the same way Scottie and Kruger had.

"Would your brother-in-law do something like this?" I asked.

"With billions of dollars at stake, not to mention it would be Baltasar's heirs who would control Santoval from now on…" She didn't finish the sentence. Clearly, though, she believed he was capable.

"What is the current relationship between Leandro and his brother?" Rile asked.

"They are cordial but never turn their back to each other. Metaphorically speaking, of course."

When Rile's cell phone rang, he excused himself to take the call, which had to mean whatever it was, was urgent. He returned a few minutes later.

"Does Santoval own a private jet?" he asked.

"They own several," Amanda responded.

"Have you ever heard of *Activos Comerciales de Mallorca LLC*?"

"I have not." She hesitated just long enough that, coupled with the way her expression had changed when Rile asked the question, I was certain she was lying. My eyes met his, and I could tell he concurred, especially when she checked her phone and her brow furrowed. "Leandro will be concerned about my being away so long."

"Before you go, I'd like to circle back to who might have a motive to kidnap your son," said Rile.

She looked at him and nodded. "Go ahead."

"You mentioned Baltasar. Besides your brother-in-law, can you think of anyone else?"

"The life we lead—the money, the power, enemies both from within Santoval and from competitors—the threat of kidnapping and extortion is one we've lived with since Tres was born. Even before that. It's one of the reasons my husband and I have led a private life."

"I would expect, if your brother-in-law is not behind it, the kidnappers will be contacting your husband about a ransom," said Rile. "We would like to set up a means to monitor incoming calls in the event you receive one."

"I don't know…"

"Excuse me?" Did she just say she didn't know?

"My husband is a very private man."

Rile studied her, brushing his lower lip with his finger. "If you prefer, I am willing to speak with him directly."

"That won't be necessary. I'll talk to him, and if he agrees, I'll let you know."

I felt anger building. Did she not understand what was at stake here? We were talking about the life of her only child. "Amanda, if Baltasar is behind Tres' disappearance, what do you think he'll do?"

"He will kill my son, if he hasn't already."

"And any other kidnapper? What do you think they'll do once they've received their ransom demand?"

"I don't know," she repeated.

A chill spread throughout my body, and I began to shake from both fear and anger. "Then, how can you or your husband not agree to everything humanly possible to find Tres?" Knowing, if I didn't leave the room, I'd say something worse than I already had, I stormed outside and over to the path that led down to the beach.

"I'm sorry," I said to Rile when he joined me a few minutes later.

He embraced me. "Your reaction was appropriate. Hers was not."

"Is she gone?"

"Yes."

I took a step back when Rile dropped his arms.

"I need to do something. I can't just wait around to hear either from the kidnappers or Decker or both."

"I have news from one front." Rile led me over to the same boulders we sat on the other day. "I received word from Deck. He has been looking into flights departing from the Austin airfield as well as DFW and Houston on the day Tres went missing."

"And?"

"A flight plan was filed for a private aircraft leaving Houston at sixteen hundred hours, traveling to Madrid."

My eyes opened wide. "Is that why you asked if Santoval owned a plane? Was it one of theirs?"

"It was not. The aircraft is owned by the same LLC as the house in Las Vegas and in Austin." Rile's phone rang. "This is Decker again," he said before answering and asking if he could return the call once we were inside.

"Two things," Decker began once we were gathered at the table where Vex, Scottie, and Kruger waited and Rile had put the call on speaker. "First, according to flight logs, the plane I told you we tracked out of Houston the day Tres disappeared hasn't left Madrid. Second, I dug deeper into who's behind *Activos Comerciales de Mallorca*. He sure as hell didn't make it easy."

"He?" I asked.

"Tres."

"Tres owns the LLC?" I gasped.

"Correct, although he tried to bury it under a mountain of misleading information. He obviously never thought he'd be up against the likes of me."

"Are you saying you think Tres left of his own accord and flew to Madrid?" I asked.

"Either that or Tres' kidnappers used his own plane to transport him out of the country."

"Are there any other parties listed on the LLC?" Rile asked.

"Sure enough. A guy by the name of Alejandro Barello. Tres' cousin."

"Do you have a photo of him?"

"Yes, ma'am. Just messaged it to you."

I looked at my phone's screen. As I anticipated, Alejandro, Tres' cousin, was the same man I'd met in Las Vegas.

"Do you have any leads on where he might be?" Vex asked.

"Workin' on that now," Decker responded.

"I have a somewhat unrelated question," I said.

"Go ahead," said Decker at the same time Rile told me to proceed.

"Since Tres didn't bother to use an alias when he left Spain, how was it his background check didn't have any information about his family or where he lived prior to his moving to Las Vegas?"

"Easy answer. The background checks Hammer ran on all the Long Branch employees had a specific purpose, and that was to look for red flags regarding employment. Tres' had none; thus, a more in-depth look wasn't necessary. I can tell you the one I've run since includes everything down to how much he weighed when he was twelve years old."

"Does anyone have further questions?" Rile asked.

"Not at this time," I responded. Everyone else shook their heads.

"I'm still working on getting security footage both from the airfield in Houston and in Madrid. I'll let you know as soon as we do," said Decker before ending the call.

I folded my hands in front of me and rested them on the table. "Scottie? Kruger? Do either of you have any comments?" Both of them had spent the majority of the meeting with Amanda watching and listening.

"Some of Tres' mother's reactions were off," said Scottie.

"Agreed," said Kruger. "She's hiding something."

Vex nodded but didn't say anything.

"What happens next?" Kruger asked.

"While we wait to hear from Decker, we will begin our investigation of Baltasar Barello," Rile responded, looking directly at Scottie, who nodded.

Given Tres had been abducted while in the United States, the FBI—her current employer—had jurisdiction over the crime in conjunction with the Department of Homeland Security, her former employer. Of every-one in the room presently, she was the best person to initiate the investigation into Tres' uncle as well as lead it.

It had been four days since I left Tres sleeping in my bed and came home later to discover him missing. As with any kidnapping, time was of the essence.

As Amanda's words, "He will kill my son, if he hasn't already," played over and over in my head, I prayed we weren't already too late.

18

Tres

I wasn't exactly certain how many days had passed—but I guessed four or five—since I was abducted from Ellison's house not long after she'd left for a meeting. Before I realized what was happening, men had entered the bedroom while I was sleeping, put a bag over my head, bound my arms and legs, and carried me out. From there, I was transported some distance by car, then transferred to an aircraft.

I wouldn't be surprised if the plane ride that followed brought me to Mallorca. If not there specifically, at least to Spain.

At some point during the flight, I was given an injection that knocked me out. When I woke, I was in the same small room I was in now. The bag that had been over my head as well as the ropes that kept me bound had been removed.

While my accommodations were not luxurious by any means, I had a reasonably comfortable bed and an en-suite lavatory. Only one door separated me from the rest of the building I was being held captive in. Even the door between the bedroom and the bathroom had been removed from its hinges. Neither room had windows, making it impossible for me to know whether it was day or night.

In the time since I was brought here, I hadn't seen another person or heard anyone speak. Food and water were delivered to me through a small opening that had been cut in the bottom of the bedroom door, which appeared to be blocked by a steel plate when not in use.

Even the timing of the meals was designed to keep me unaware of the hour. Breakfast foods would be served several meals in a row, then they'd switch to other fare. Meals were sometimes served within minutes of each other, and sometimes it was hours between them.

As far as who was behind my abduction, I had two theories. The first and most obvious was my father. But if it was him, why was I being held captive?

I knew what he wanted from me, and that was to return to Mallorca and my position as CEO of the Santoval Group. Did he think the kidnapping and subsequent imprisonment would be so terrifying I would agree to anything he asked once I was free? It seemed illogical.

While my father could be a bastard of epic proportions, he had also been raised in the lap of luxury and given everything he'd ever wanted. It would make more sense if he'd had me abducted, then flown to Mallorca and delivered to him. Once there, I had no doubt he would have insisted the time for game playing was over and demanded I take the helm of Santoval as he had before me and his father had before him.

If this theory was the correct one, he'd gone to a great deal of trouble for nothing. I'd already decided to return to Mallorca. Except, instead of returning to do his bidding, it would be to confront him about his deceit and manipulation.

When I'd agreed to step in as CEO, my understanding was it would only be until such time as my father's health improved enough for him to return. After a few weeks, my mother had approached me, saying she felt obligated to tell me the truth—that it was all a ruse to get me to do something I'd vowed never to do.

It was her idea that I travel to the United States and remain in hiding until my father finally realized the rules of succession for the Santoval Group had to change. Either that, or it would end up under the control of his brother, Baltasar—something my father would never allow to happen if there was any way he could prevent it.

The next day, Alejandro, my cousin and Baltasar's oldest son, and I left Mallorca. Had he remained, Alejandro would've been stuck in the same way I was, a pawn in our fathers' battle for control of the Santoval Group.

There was never any doubt my dad would move heaven and earth to find me and force me to return. When I was in Las Vegas with Ellison and Alejandro had interrupted our lovemaking, saying he'd received a message from *La Pequeña Gorrión*—the little Sparrow—he was speaking about my mother. She'd been helping Alejandro and me stay one step ahead of my father since we left Mallorca.

Once I met Ellison, though, I knew my days of running had to come to an end. I had to settle things with him once and for all so I was free to live whatever life she and I chose for ourselves.

I'd informed Alejandro of my plan to return to Mallorca and what I planned to do. The only holdup was I hadn't yet confessed to Ellison who I really was.

I'd intended to do so the day I was kidnapped. After we'd chosen our wedding rings, I was prepared to ask her to travel to Mallorca with me.

That I'd been taken against my will *might* mean my father had found me before I had the chance to return on my own.

My other theory was my uncle, Baltasar, was behind the kidnapping. If that was the case, I couldn't help but wonder why I was still alive. The fastest way for him to get what I knew he wanted—permanent control of the Santoval Group—would be to kill me. With my father's health issues and me out of the picture, it was easy to imagine the board would unanimously vote to hand the family business over to him and his heirs.

I feared if this theory was the correct one, Alejandro, who besides being my cousin was one of my closest friends and trusted allies, might be in danger himself, given he would do everything in his power not to allow his father's coup to take place. In fact, he may very well have been abducted too and was being held either here, where I was, or at another location.

There was only one way I could think of to force the issue—force my captors to reveal themselves—and that would be to make them believe I was about to kill myself.

If my father was behind my abduction, they would rush in to stop me. If my uncle was, they would either run in to finish me off or leave me alone to do the deed myself.

So far, I'd only come up with one idea to do this, and it wasn't a very good one. Since I had no doubt there was a camera monitoring me, perhaps more than one, the trickiest part of my plan would be to figure out how to make a noose from the bed sheets and determine a way to use it to hang myself—all without them seeing what I was up to ahead of time.

I lay on the bed and closed my eyes, trying to think up a better plan. Instead, my mind drifted, as it always did, to Ellison, my wife, the love of my life, the person who, in only a few short days, came to matter more to me than anyone else.

Perhaps, instead of pretending I was about to kill myself, a better plan would be to attempt to make a deal with whoever was guarding me. If I did, I would first have to flip a metaphoric coin to determine which of my theories was correct.

If my father was my captor, I would promise that, if I was released, I would return to Santoval.

If it was my uncle, I'd promise to disappear from the face of the earth and never reappear as long as he let me live out the rest of my life with my wife.

Regardless of which deal I chose to attempt to make, I could only pray Ellison loved me enough to stand by me if I was successful.

19

Fury

"What about setting up monitoring in case a ransom call comes in?" Kruger asked as we waited to hear something from Decker.

"It is already in place." While Rile responded, he didn't look at the man who'd asked the question. He brushed his lower lip with his fingertip, picked up his phone with his other hand, and swiped the screen.

"How?" I asked.

"I took care of it the other night," he answered but still seemed distracted.

"What's going on, Rile?"

"I am anxious to see what Amanda does next."

"Did you intentionally ask the two questions about whether Santoval owned a plane and if she was familiar with the LLC back to back?"

Rile nodded.

"Do you have someone tailing her?"

"In a manner of speaking."

"You had a device put on her car?"

Rile nodded a second time. "It does not appear she intends to return to the Barello estate." Rile set his phone on the table and turned his laptop so we could all see it.

"Is she headed to the airport?" I watched the indicator for her vehicle as it moved in that direction. A second indicator appeared not far behind her. "Who's that?"

"Pedro," Rile responded.

I clenched my fists under the table as my mind raced with what her destination might mean. Was she on her way to the airfield to see if Tres' plane was there? If so, why? And if the two questions Rile had asked were the reason for her bizarre reaction to him suggesting incoming calls be monitored, why not share her concerns with us in the same way she had everything else?

I clenched my fists under the table in frustration. All I wanted was what I believed she wanted too—to find Tres.

"Now you're here, we will find my son together," was the first thing she'd said when she arrived earlier. What had changed?

I groaned in frustration.

"Do not jump to conclusions yet," said Rile, covering my hand with his.

"If only I had conclusions to jump to," I muttered.

"Perhaps soon," he responded.

"Something about the plane set her off," said Vex, standing and walking over to look out the window. "Was it some clue as to Tres' whereabouts?"

"If so, why would she pursue it alone? Wouldn't she want our help?" Scottie asked.

"Not if she believed Tres staged his disappearance," I seethed under my breath. If I found out he had, our marriage would be over. The worry, the fear, the betrayal would all be too much for me to overcome.

My eyes met Vex's, and he shook his head. "If that were his plan, he would've asked you to go with him."

"I agree," added Scottie.

"Not that anyone asked, but I think so too," said Kruger.

I rested my elbows on the table and rubbed my temples with the tips of my fingers. "Here's what we know. Tres disappeared the morning after our wedding while I was away at a meeting. He and I had agreed to shop for wedding rings that afternoon."

"The house where you stayed in Las Vegas was emptied out less than twenty-four hours after we returned to Texas. For all intents and purposes, it appears Alejandro is missing too," added Vex.

"Tres' mother believes he's in danger, but for some reason, she doesn't appear to want her husband to know." That in itself made no sense to me. I could understand why she wouldn't share Tres' whereabouts with him after they'd argued and Tres left, but he was their only son. Wouldn't she want his father to know Tres was in danger?

"Or she doesn't want her husband to know she knows," said Vex.

My head shot up. "Do you think Leandro is responsible for his son's kidnapping?"

"It's one possibility."

I nodded. If that was the case, I couldn't fathom Leandro harming his son. Maybe he'd want to frighten him.

If Vex was right, it meant Leandro and Amanda didn't trust or confide in one another. I shook my head. Did Tres think that kind of relationship was normal? Is that why he hadn't told me about his family? I couldn't live that way. I wouldn't live that way.

"Let's take a walk," said Rile, motioning me outside.

"I'd rather not."

"Please."

Like before, we walked over to the path that led down to the beach.

"I know what you are thinking."

When I cocked my head and smirked, Rile smiled.

"We will find Tres, and when we do, I beg you to give him the chance to explain."

"Why is it so important to you, Rile?"

"To find love is a rare and wonderful gift, Ellison. I speak from experience."

"It seems as though a lot of the Invincibles would agree. Maybe that's why I got caught up in it. I don't even know Tres."

"Give him a chance; that is all I ask of you."

I heard Vex whistle and looked behind me to see him waving us in.

"Pedro said Amanda drove to a hangar located at the private airfield adjacent to the Palma airport," he said once we were closer. "She used a key to enter, was inside only a few seconds, then returned to her car and left. It appears she's headed home."

Why had she gone to the hangar? I couldn't think of a logical reason.

Rile's cell rang. He put the call on speaker without asking first. "Hello, Decker," he said.

"Hey, I'm initiating video conferencing. This old-school phone crap is gettin' on my nerves."

We went inside, and Rile opened the laptop and positioned it so we could all see Decker.

"That's better. So listen, I was able to get my hands on security footage from the airfield in Madrid. It's grainy and taken from some distance. However, it shows the plane I mentioned before being pulled inside a hangar. Five minutes later, an SUV arrived and went in as well. Fast forward another ten minutes, and the SUV leaves in a big hurry. We're trying to isolate audio now, but if my hunch is right, what we're hearing are gunshots."

My legs gave out, and I would've fallen if Vex hadn't caught me. Kruger pulled a chair out from the table, and I sat down. Scottie brought me a glass of water, which I refused.

"Fury?" Decker asked. "You okay?"

"Yes, sir. Sorry."

He shook his head. "I'm the one who should apologize for my blunt delivery. Anyway, Scottie? You there?"

"Yes, sir." She'd picked up her phone after setting the glass of water down.

"What do you have in the way of reinforcements in Madrid?" he asked.

"Working that now, sir. I should have a team at my disposal within the hour."

"Good deal. It'll take you about ninety minutes to get there. Rile, you got a plane handy?"

If I didn't know better, I would've thought I'd caught Rile rolling his eyes. "Yes, Ashford. We'll take the Bombardier."

"Sweet. I always loved that plane."

"I'll remind you the aircraft is my personal property as opposed to an Invincibles asset."

"Yeah, yeah. All I'm sayin' is maybe we'll add one to the US fleet."

I knew the two were teasing, and given Decker's belief he could hear gunshots in the security footage from the hangar, I appreciated the momentary distraction.

"Give me a holler when you land in Madrid. By then, I'll have sent you the coordinates of the hangar."

"Roger that," said Rile, ending the video chat. He looked directly at me.

"I'm going along," I said before he could either ask or suggest otherwise.

When Vex, Scottie, Kruger, and I arrived at the hangar, a team was already inside, gathering evidence. Scottie said she would check in with them first before the rest of us entered.

I leaned against the SUV, folded my arms, and lifted my face to the sun. I might be in a state of either shock or denial, but my gut was telling me Tres was still alive. Even after Scottie returned, saying she believed there were at least two victims of what appeared to have been a gunfight. "Looks like there are casings from both a .357 and a .44 magnum. Too much blood for both victims to have survived. The other may have gotten away with a lesser wound."

I bent at the waist and took several deep breaths. Someone was dead, but I'd bet my own life it wasn't Tres. That's how powerful the feelings I had were.

I raised my head when I heard someone holler Scottie's name. As she rushed over, I saw an agent point toward a part of the hangar I couldn't see from where I stood.

I entered after her, slowly walking in the direction I saw Scottie and the other agent go. I was about to round a corner when she intercepted me.

"What's back there?" I asked.

"A body."

"Whose?"

"The team is working on a positive ID, but I can say with some certainty it's Alejandro Barello."

I felt dizzy, but was able to remain calm by taking a few deep breaths. "Let me ID him."

"Are you certain you want to do that?" asked Vex. "Any of us could."

"I want to do it," I insisted. Scottie led the way to where one of the agents was covering the body with a sheet. The man looked up when we approached and moved aside.

"That's him." I turned around and walked over to another area where one team of agents was gathering casings near the plane's airstairs. I looked across the space to where a different team was doing the same.

"There's a door on that side," said Vex. "The killer must've entered through it and started firing. It appears he got quite a few shots off."

"There are more casings over there," said Kruger, pointing to the right of a door marked as an exit. "Different caliber."

"Looks like they came from near the door where the SUV would've come in," said Vex.

Scottie approached. "Have you developed a theory?" she asked him.

"Most logical scenario is Tres was led off the plane when the gunman came in through the side door. Alejandro was able to get several shots off before he got hit."

"The coroner and medical examiner are here now. While they're not ready to make it official, they said it appears only one shot hit him. Unfortunately, it was fatal," said Scottie.

The four of us walked over to the exit door. "There are only traces of blood over here," I said, following Vex outside.

"There's a trail that leads over here," he said, pointing to the ground. "Then it stops."

"The assailant killed Alejandro, got hit himself, and took off." I looked around the area for security cameras. While I didn't immediately see one, it didn't mean there weren't any. "Send Decker footage of this entire area," I said to Kruger. "See if he can get his hands on any other security feeds."

"Roger that." While he took several photos from every direction, Vex and I followed Scottie inside.

"How you doin'?" he asked.

"Tres is still alive," I blurted.

Vex nodded. "I think so too." He put his arm around my shoulders and pulled me into a brotherly embrace. "We're gonna find him, Fury. I can feel it. And it's gonna be soon."

After taking several more walks around the interior and exterior of the hangar, Vex asked if I was ready to return to Mallorca.

I shook my head. "I'm not leaving Madrid until we're certain Tres is no longer here."

He nodded. "Copy that."

"I've made arrangements for us to stay in an apartment in Madrid Centro," said Scottie. "It's quite large, so it can accommodate all of us, and it's a five-minute walk from the bureau's international field office."

"Distance from the airfield?" I asked.

"About eighteen kilometers."

So roughly ten miles. I wasn't sure there'd be a reason for us to return to the hangar, but if there was, it was close enough to where we'd be staying.

"What about notification of next of kin?" Kruger asked.

Scottie nodded. "Tomorrow."

I hadn't thought about that when I said I wasn't leaving Madrid. "I changed my mind. I'm going with you or whoever handles the notification." If Baltasar had any connection to Tres' kidnapping, I wanted to be there when he received the news his oldest son was dead.

"Me too," said Vex.

"It's almost like a small-scale gang war," Kruger said once we were in the SUV on our way into the Centro District.

I reflected on a conversation I'd had with Rile before I came to Mallorca. I'd asked him if Tres had a cousin by the name of Alejandro, and he'd said he would attempt to find out if Tres had a close ally within Santoval with that name. I remembered being stunned by his word choice.

"Family businesses as large as Santoval often operate with opposing sides," I said, paraphrasing Rile's words that day.

He'd gone on to say if we discovered someone within Tres' own family was responsible for his disappearance, it wouldn't come as a surprise.

Now, it seemed I'd be more shocked if whoever was responsible was from outside his family.

20

Fury

Instead of waiting until the next morning to return to Mallorca, Rile suggested we travel that night, given there'd be a better chance of finding Baltasar at home in order to notify him of his son's death.

"What about Alejandro's mother?" I asked when he called.

"Valentina Barello passed away fifteen years ago," Rile responded. "It is my understanding he and Tres grew close during that time."

"Did Alejandro spend a lot of time with Tres' family?"

"I believe so, but like everything else with the Barellos, there are few who know and fewer who speak of it if they do."

"Who lives with Baltasar now?" I remembered Rile saying he and his wife had seven children. My guess was Alejandro was close to Tres' age, which was twenty-nine or thirty. That meant the woman had given birth every other year on average. It also meant Alejandro would have at least one sibling still in his or her teens.

I heard Kensington say something in the background, but I couldn't make out exactly what.

"My wife said the two youngest, Orlando and Paloma, live with their father."

"Does she know much about the other siblings?" I asked.

"Perhaps it would be easier if you spoke directly."

When Rile put the call on speaker, Kensington said Alejandro's next oldest sibling was his sister Eliana. After that was Pascual, then another boy named Raymon and another girl named Renata.

"Eliana and Pascual are the only two who I believe work for Santoval," said Rile.

"Eliana is older than Pascual, then?"

"That is correct."

And yet, now that Alejandro was dead, if Santoval somehow wound up under the leadership of Baltasar, Eliana would be passed over as heir.

I rested my head against the seat and closed my eyes after ending the call. Had it been my fate to be born into a family like the Barellos, I probably would've been disowned before I reached my teenage years. According to my mother, I had never been shy about offering my opinion and often bested the boys in most sports when I was still in elementary school. That, coupled with my temper—Leandro, Baltasar, or their equivalent, never would've known what hit them.

It was shortly after nine when we pulled up to the gate of Baltasar Barello's estate behind the escort provided by the local *policía.*

"He isn't doing too bad for being the second son," Kruger muttered.

I had to agree. While not on the scale of Leandro and Amanda's home, this one was grander on the outside than most I'd visited in my life.

"¿Qué es esto?" Baltasar barked when we arrived at the front door, which I guessed meant, "what is this about?"

"We have an urgent matter to discuss with you, sir," Scottie responded in English. "May we please step inside?"

He left the door open, and we followed.

"Please have a seat," said Vex.

Baltasar glared at him.

"Please, sir."

Baltasar sat.

"Sir, we're here to talk to you about your son Alejandro," Scottie began.

"My son and I do not speak."

"Yes, sir."

While we'd agreed on the way over that Scottie would be the one to deliver the news, when she turned to Vex, he took a step forward. "Sir, I am sorry to inform you that Alejandro is dead."

It was as though all the air had left the room as we waited for Baltasar to process the news. No one spoke, including him, for several seconds.

"Papa?" I heard a female voice say from behind me. I turned around, and a teenage girl stood, waiting for her father's response. I was about to walk over to her to offer comfort when I heard his voice.

"*¡Tú, a tu cuarto!*" he shouted, telling her to go to her room.

"But—"

"*¡Tú, a tu cuarto!*" he repeated, pointing behind her.

The girl, who I assumed was Paloma, ran toward and up the stairs.

After she disappeared from view, I looked in Baltasar's direction. He'd become a different man in those few seconds. He was hunched forward with his head in his hands. "What happened?"

Vex stepped closer and sat in the adjacent chair. "The details aren't entirely clear yet, but your son was shot, sir. It appears there may have been a gun battle with at least one other person, but perhaps more."

"Where?" Baltasar's head was still in his hands, so I couldn't see his expression. However, his voice that had been angry when we arrived, now sounded anguished.

"At a private plane hangar in Madrid."

Baltasar looked up. "Were there other fatalities?"

"No, but we do believe one other person may have been injured in the altercation."

Baltasar's eyes appeared unfocused, staring straight ahead, glazed over. The slow nod of his head was almost imperceptible.

"Sir, I understand this has come as a shock, and we'll give you your privacy now. However, we'd like to make arrangements to speak with you in greater detail tomorrow about what happened."

Baltasar stood, walked over, and opened the front door. "Call my office."

As we filed out, my eyes met his. Neither of us looked away for what felt like minutes but, in actuality, was only a few seconds. When he turned his head, I followed Vex and Scottie out to the SUV.

No one spoke on the drive to Rile's compound, and when we arrived, I walked to the Whitby guesthouse without saying as much as good night.

The next morning, I received a message from Rile, inviting me to the main house for breakfast. Instead of heading there right away, I made myself a cup of tea and sat by the window, looking out at the Bay of Palma. The sun's reflection on the crisp blue water was bright, but the skies might as well have been clouded over with as dark and desperate as I felt.

I hadn't really known Alejandro besides how gracious he was to me, but if he and Tres were as close as everyone said they were, his death would hit my husband hard.

"Where are you, Tres?" I cried as tears rolled down my cheeks. *"Where the fuck are you?"*

I wasn't sure how long I'd been sitting in the chair, staring out the window at nothing, when I heard a knock.

"Coming," I said, standing and tightening my robe around me.

When I pulled the door open, Vex was standing on the other side.

"You okay?" he asked.

"I think I already said this, but I don't think I'll be okay again until we find Tres."

"Completely understandable."

I took a step back. "Do you want to come in?"

He shook his head. "Rile said Decker found something for us to follow up on."

My eyes opened wide. "Vex! What the hell? Why didn't you lead with that?" I raced to the other side of the room, grabbing clothes as I went.

"See you at the main house," he said, shutting the door behind him.

I grabbed my phone and looked at the screen. "Shit," I muttered. I'd missed two calls and as many messages from Rile. Thank God he'd sent Vex to check on me. When I read them again, I was relieved to see only ten minutes had passed between the first and now.

"What did Decker find?" I asked, not caring that I'd interrupted a conversation when I ran in the back door of Rile's house.

"What he believes is footage of the SUV that was at the hangar in Madrid," Rile responded.

"Which one?"

His head cocked. "Was there more than one?"

"Never mind. Where?"

"He tracked it to *Barrio de las Letras*," said Rile. He pulled up a map. "This is where it last appeared on security footage. As you can see, the streets in the area are closed off except for the—"

"Does Decker think this is where Tres is?" I interrupted.

"Yes."

I looked over at Vex. "Let's *go!*"

He stood, as did Scottie and Kruger.

"We have a visitor," Rile said, swiping the screen of his cell. "Amanda Barello has just come through the gate."

"I can't explain why, but I don't want her to know Tres might be in Madrid yet."

"It's your call," said Vex when Rile nodded.

"Is it?"

"He's your husband, Fury," said Scottie.

"Right. So, yeah, it's my call, and we need to leave."

The same modest car Amanda previously arrived in pulled through the gate. She parked, cut the engine, and got out. Her hair was as disheveled as her clothes, and when she pulled the sunglasses off her face, her red-rimmed eyes were bloodshot. "Do you have any news about my son?" she asked.

"Not yet," Kruger responded. He approached, took her arm, and led her toward the house as I stood, unable to speak. "Why don't we go inside?"

She looked over her shoulder at me. "But—"

"Rile and I will explain as much as we know once we're inside," said Kruger, motioning us in the opposite direction with his head.

"Should we—"

"Come on," said Vex, tugging my arm after interrupting me. "Rile will handle it."

Scottie drove to the airfield while Vex and I reviewed everything Decker had sent over. I understood why it had taken so long for him to piece together what he believed was the SUV's route that night. In certain images, I wasn't sure myself it was the same vehicle.

We'd just boarded Rile's Bombardier when a vehicle pulled up on the tarmac. Kruger jumped out and raced over.

"Damn, that was rough," he said as we climbed the airstairs and took our seats on the plane. "In addition to asking about Tres several more times, she also asked if we'd been able to locate Alejandro. Rile was the one to tell her we hadn't."

"Sorry we left you there. I misunderstood."

Kruger shook his head. "No, I wanted you to be able to leave. Rile finally got me out of there. I wasn't sure I'd make it before you took off."

"How is she?" I asked.

Kruger took the seat next to me and shook his head. "A complete wreck." He dropped his head and shook it. "The hardest part was she kept crying and repeating how she was afraid she'd never find Tres. Maybe I shouldn't tell you that, but, man, it was heart-wrenching."

My eyes filled with tears, empathizing with her. But I *believed* Tres was alive. I wouldn't stop searching for him, and neither would Vex, Scottie, or Kruger.

"What are you thinking?" Vex asked.

"We aren't going to stop until we find him."

"Damn straight," Kruger said, taking my hand and squeezing it.

"Let's look at photos from *Barrio de las Letras*," said Vex, taking a seat across from his brother and me.

The area, which translated to the Literary Quarter, was known for its narrow streets with restricted access to vehicles. The SUV Decker traced had pulled into an alleyway near the intersection of Calle del Léon and Calle del Infante. That had been the last footage of it he could locate.

The block it disappeared in appeared to be no more than a tenth of a mile long. On the street level, there was a theater, one restaurant with a youth hostel above it, and several other shops and restaurants with three to four floors of apartments above them.

"There are a few shots of alleyways in the area but none specifically of the one the SUV went down," said Vex.

I got up and sat beside him. "What is that?" I asked, pointing to one.

"It looks like it might be one of those rolling garage doors. Although it seems unlikely, that's what it is."

Scottie looked up from her own computer. "Some of the apartment buildings in the quarter are quite luxurious. There are one or two for sale that list parking as an amenity."

Until we arrived and walked the block, there was no way of knowing if there were any. The other thing we didn't know was whether the SUV drove down it, then to another without security camera coverage.

"Here's one," said Scottie, turning her laptop so Vex and I could see the screen.

"Would you send that to me?" I asked.

"Of course. I have four agents on the ground there now, just getting the lay of the land. Do you want them to take more photos?"

"Everything they can in the block. Back and front of the buildings lining the alleyway on either side."

"You got it."

"Is there anything specific I can help you look for?" Vex asked when I returned to the seat beside him.

"Tres."

I couldn't explain it, and I knew it sounded far-fetched, but when I'd looked at the images on the screen while we were on the plane and now that we were standing at the same intersection the SUV had turned off of, I *knew* Tres was here. It was as though I could feel him the same way Rile had told me he knew Kensington was several yards behind us, up on a balcony, without even looking. "When your true love is near, you will feel their presence long before you see them," he'd said.

I could *feel* Tres, just not strongly enough to know exactly where to look.

21

Tres

I stared down at the plate of chicken and rice that had been delivered a few minutes ago, then picked up the knife and fork resting next to it on the tray. I cut into the piece of chicken, wondering if the blade would be sharp enough for me to use to cut myself. Perhaps, but not enough to do the kind of damage a staged suicide attempt would require. Neither would stabbing myself with the fork.

I cut a second piece of the meat and had another thought. I brought the fork to my mouth, chewed for a couple of seconds, then jumped up from the bed where I'd been sitting, turned my back to the door, and clutched my throat, wheezing and coughing as though I was choking.

I kept up the charade when I heard the door open and someone come in. When he got close enough, I slammed my head back as hard as I could, then reached between my legs and grabbed the back of his knee. I pulled it toward me with as much force as I could. When the man fell to the ground, unconscious and with blood pouring from his nose, I grabbed the gun he had in his hand. I thought about killing him for a split second but changed my mind and shot out one kneecap instead, then raced out the bedroom door.

I kept the gun pointed and ready to shoot, figuring another captor would have heard the shot, but I encountered no one as I looked around the one other room of an apartment with floor-to-ceiling windows. I raced over to one that looked like it opened to a small patio. Once close enough, I realized that, instead of a patio, it was a fire escape.

I stuck the gun I'd taken from my captor in the back of my pants and climbed down as quickly as I could. There was no time for me to survey the area to try to figure out where I was; I couldn't afford a misstep that would send me plummeting three, then two, then just one story to the ground below me. I jumped from the final landing.

"*¿Dónde estoy?*" I said to the people walking near the end of an alleyway. "*Where am I?*" I shouted again but, this time, in English.

"Loco puto Americano," grumbled an old man who shuffled his feet more than walked.

He could call me a crazy fucking American all day long as long as he told me where I was. *"¿Dónde estoy?"* I repeated.

"Barrio de las Letras."

Something told me to turn and go the other way rather than out to the main thoroughfare. As I did, I blinked my eyes several times, imagining I saw *mi tormenta* staring up at the building on the opposite side of the fire escape I'd just come down. When I blinked again and she was still there, I called her name as I walked toward her.

"Ellison?"

"Tres!" she screamed, running—not walking—to me. I did the same. When we met, I picked her up and spun her in a circle.

I set her feet on the ground and put my hands on either side of her face. "Am I dreaming? How are you here? Why are you here?"

Tears streamed down her face. "Looking for you. I'm here looking for you."

When I heard the screech of tires behind me, I spun around, reaching for the gun.

"Tres! Stop!" Ellison cried. "That's Vex. Come on."

She grabbed my hand, and we ran toward the SUV, climbing into the open door of the backseat and shutting it behind us as it raced off.

I had a million questions, none of which mattered now. Like in the alley, I put my hands on either side of my beloved wife's face and stared into her eyes. "I love you, Ellison Barello."

"I love you, Tres Barello."

I lowered my mouth to hers and kissed her the way I promised myself I would if I lived long enough to see her again.

"This is only a little uncomfortable," I heard the guy sitting beside me on the bench seat mutter. I ignored him and continued kissing Ellison until the SUV stopped and the engine cut.

"Damn, ten minutes without breathing. I've never seen anything like it," joked the man I recognized as Kruger Dunning as he opened the back passenger door and got out.

When I turned back to look at Ellison, tears streamed down her cheeks.

"Mi tormenta," I whispered as I kissed each one away.

"Come on, you two," said Vex. "I'm sure you'd much rather be somewhere you can be alone."

When we got out, I realized we were in front of the nicest hotel in all of Madrid.

"You're in the penthouse," said Vex, handing me the key card envelope. "Unless you'd rather—"

"There is nothing I'd rather do," I said, looking into Ellison's still-tearful eyes. "You?"

She shook her head and smiled. "Nothing."

"¡Dios mío!" Something occurred to me.

"What?" Ellison gasped.

"The man who was guarding me. I shot him. He's…" I hadn't paid attention to the location of the apartment in my rush to escape. Then, when I saw *mi tormenta* standing in the alley, all other thoughts had left my mind.

"He's what, Tres?"

"I do not remember where I was." I closed my eyes, trying to picture it. "It was across from where you were standing. I came down the fire escape. It was on the fourth floor."

"Got it," said Vex. "Scottie, you stay here at the hotel and make sure security is set up everywhere we discussed. Kruger and I will go back and look for this guy."

"I know there is so much for us to talk about," I said once we were alone in the elevator. While I'd gotten lost in Ellison's embrace, thinking about the man I'd shot reminded me my entire life was in upheaval.

"Not yet, Tres," Ellison said, wrapping her arms around me and resting her head on my chest. "There is plenty of time to talk tomorrow. Now, I need to make love to my husband."

"And I need to make love to my wife."

The elevator stopped and opened to a small foyer with only one door. Once inside the suite, the first thing I wanted to do was peel off the clothes I'd been wearing for the last several days, then burn them.

My *Fury*, my love, my *tormenta*, watched as I removed every stitch. When I stood naked before her, she walked over and rested her hands on my chest, then kissed both my cheeks.

"Come with me," she said, leading me into one of the bedrooms, then into the bathroom. She turned the water on and began filling the tub. "Are you hungry?" she asked.

"Only for you, *mi amor*." I watched her peel off her clothes just as she'd watched me, taking in every inch of the body I'd feared I'd never see again, never hold again, never make love to again.

She turned the water off, climbed in, and held out her hand for me to join her.

I sank into the hot water and closed my eyes, focused only on how my wife's hands felt as she washed me like I'd done for her so often in the short time we were together. Now that we had a lifetime to care for one another, I planned to nurture and love her every minute of every day.

I dipped my head into the water after she'd lathered my hair with shampoo. "Let me take care of you now, Ellison," I said, sitting up.

She shifted from her knees to her bottom, resting against the opposite side of the bathtub. I soaped my hands, then beginning with her neck, trailed my fingers down her nakedness. I spread her legs and knelt between them, leaning forward to kiss her neck, where my hands had been. When I fingered her nipples and she moaned, desire shot through me like a bolt of lightning. I wanted to take things slow, make love to her for hours, but the need I felt was so powerful I couldn't deny it. I shifted her body so I could gather Ellison in my arms, stood, and walked out of the bathroom and over to the bed, both of us dripping wet.

"I cannot wait, my love." My heart beat madly as I spread her legs. *"Niña hermosa,"* I groaned as I lowered myself and put my mouth on her pussy. I put one hand on her breast, the stiff peak of her nipple poking into my palm, and with the other, I let my fingers glide through her wetness.

When Ellison pleaded with me for more, I took one of her hands and moved it to her breast, like mine had been. I placed the other between her legs.

"Touch yourself," I demanded. "Feel how much you want me."

I settled my mouth between her fingers that were toying with her clit, pressed my tongue against the bud, then lapped at her, first slow, then quickening. When I felt her clench, I sucked—hard—until my beautiful, passionate, exquisite storm cried out my name in pleasure.

Before she had a chance to come down from her peak of ecstasy, I thrust my hardness where my tongue had been, slamming myself into her with all the pent-up passion, desire, and need I felt for her. Ellison undulated against me, and as she let herself topple once again over the cliff of her orgasm, I kissed her lips and went with her, riding it out until we were both sated, limp in a sensual haze.

I lay beside my perfect wife, my lust for her already building again. Without opening my eyes, I reached over and palmed her pussy, then ran my finger through her folds.

Her body writhed, her back arched, and she moaned for more.

I buried my fingers inside her and turned to take her straining nipple between my lips.

"I want you. In my mouth," Ellison begged. "*Please*, Tres."

I rose over her, straddled her shoulders, and fed her my cock. Her tongue swirled the tip, and her lips fastened around me, taking me into her throat.

My heart pounded in my chest, and every bit of air left my lungs. *"Ellison,"* I cried out her name as another orgasm took me as if by a raging storm. The power of it left me weak, and emotion overtook me. I moved back, leaned down, and kissed her. She opened her eyes and looked into mine.

"Tres," she whispered as she wiped tears from my cheeks. "I love you so."

22

Fury

My husband lay beside me, sleeping, as I stroked his hair and let my gaze linger on his taut, lean abdomen and the sharp edges of the muscles so clearly defined in those abs. Even in sleep, his cock was hard, and I longed to feel it inside me again and again, throughout the night and into the following day.

While I'd felt him as I walked the alleyway in *Barrio de las Letras*, I would never have dreamed that, within minutes, I'd be in his arms, his lips crashing into mine as our mouths fused to one another's as if we'd never let go.

I didn't care about the other people anxious for word of his safety. Whether Vex, Rile, or anyone else had told his mother we'd found him mattered little to me. For now, he was all mine, and I refused to let him go, even for a minute. I needed him. Not just his body; I needed his words, to hear him breathe, the beat of his heart, my name on his lips. I needed him to assure me we'd never be apart again and to confirm what his mother had said about his plans to tell me about the life he had before we met, his family, and that he'd planned to bring me to Mallorca to meet them.

I also needed to know who'd kidnapped him, so we could bring whoever it was to justice. So we could ensure those responsible were behind bars, never able to threaten him or our life together again. Perhaps the hardest thing of all would be for us to talk about our future and how he envisioned it.

He shifted to his side, rested his head on my shoulder, and nuzzled my neck. I draped my leg over his hip, and he slid his hardness deep into me. Neither of our bodies moved, but I could feel him pulse inside me.

"I love you," he whispered, reaching up to wipe away the tears that rolled down my cheeks.

"I was so scared," I whispered like he had. "So afraid I'd never see you again."

"Shh. I am here now. We are together, and we will be for the rest of our lives. Every moment of every day."

"I can't bear the thought you'll be taken from me again."

"I won't be. Whatever we have to do, however we have to live our lives, we will do it. No one will take me from you, and no one will take you from me." He cupped my breast and looked into my eyes. "I will hire a team who protects us, but we will never know they are there. Alejandro will make sure…What is it?" he asked, his eyes scrunching at the look on my face. "Did I say something wrong? Did my bringing him up remind you of our time in the pool—"

I shook my head, realizing he didn't know his cousin was dead. As hard as it would be for him, eventually, I'd need to tell him what had happened to Alejandro that night in the hangar and comfort him in his grief. But now wasn't the right time for it.

"Make love to me, Tres. I don't want to talk about anything or anyone else except you and me. Safe and in each other's arms."

He moved his hips, slowly at first, then faster and harder. I stared into his eyes, neither of us as much as blinking. With one final, powerful thrust, we both exploded. He fisted one hand in my hair. "You belong to me, Ellison," he said with a ferocity that matched the way he'd pounded into me. "You will never leave me. Do you understand?"

I reached out and touched his lips with my fingertips. "I won't leave you, Tres. I love you."

He closed his eyes momentarily, as if my words relieved him enough that he could breathe easily. While we professed our feelings and promised we'd spend the rest of our lives together, we didn't talk about the things I knew we'd need to when the sun rose in the morning.

There would be pain and sadness, endless questions, and perhaps then, some resolution. I hated the thought of telling him about Alejandro, the man it seemed he trusted more than anyone. Perhaps he'd been the only person Tres trusted—until he met me.

While I couldn't be to him what his cousin had been, I still vowed to be his safe harbor, the person he felt he could tell anything to and share everything with. I prayed it would be the kind of marriage he wanted too.

We fell asleep with our bodies joined together, arms and legs entwined, lips so close they could almost kiss.

When I woke, Tres had his head propped up on his bent arm and was studying me.

"Good morning," I said, smiling up at him and stretching my arms over my head.

"Good morning, *mi amor*." He leaned down and kissed my nose, then my cheeks, then my lips.

I rolled so we were face-to-face. "How did you sleep?"

"Good and bad. I woke myself up several times just to be sure you were beside me, then I could sleep again."

"Did you think I would leave?"

He leaned forward and kissed me. "No, I feared being with you was a dream."

I nodded and smiled. "I woke up to be sure you weren't a dream too."

Tres took my hand and kissed my palm. "But I am, no? Your dream come true?"

I laughed, and it felt like heaven. "Yes, you are definitely my dream come true."

"And handsome?"

"The handsomest man I've ever seen."

He smiled. "Ellison…my family…"

Both of us sobered.

"I've met them, Tres."

He rolled to his back and looked up at the ceiling. "My father is a *bastardo*."

I trailed my fingertip down his neck and across his clavicle. "I would have to agree."

"How did you meet?"

"I had dinner with them at their home."

Tres rolled to face me again. "Are you serious?"

I nodded. "Your mother showed me your old bedroom."

"You are telling me the truth?"

"Sure am."

He pinched his arm, and I laughed. "Are you checking to see if you're dreaming?"

"I admit I cannot even imagine such a scenario. Don't get me wrong; it makes me very happy to hear."

"But you're surprised. I get that. Just so you know, they didn't issue the invitation without some prompting."

"From?"

"The King of Spain. His nephew is someone I've known for many years—"

Tres' eyes scrunched. "How do you know him?"

I shook my head and laughed. "Oh no. Don't you dare pull the jealous boyfriend crap on me."

He raised a brow, and I laughed again.

"Sorry. I meant husband." I stopped laughing and looked into his eyes. "Either way, you're the only man I want, Tres. The only man I've ever truly wanted."

He rolled to his back again, this time pulling me so I was on top of him. "You haven't answered my question."

"Since he is happily married in the same way we are, as well as someone I have never been interested in even a little, this conversation isn't worth having. However, I will tell you I work with him. His name is Cortez DeLéon, but he goes by Rile. He's one of Decker's and Edge's partners."

"Ah, an Invincible."

"That's right."

"I do know of him, though we've never met."

"Tres, I don't know whether Vex or Scottie or even Rile has told your parents we found you. They may be waiting for your okay to do so."

His eyes scrunched. "I hope they have not. I would like to confront my father in person."

I leaned all the way forward so I could rest my body on his and my head on his chest. "Do you think he had something to do with your abduction?"

"I do. And if not him, then his brother, my uncle."

"Baltasar."

"Yes. He is Alejandro's father, who you now must know is my cousin. Not just that, he is my most trusted friend."

"I know. And I met Baltasar too."

Tres put his fingers on my chin and tilted my head so I was looking at him. "Why did you meet my uncle?"

"Tres, there's something we need to talk about. Something I need to tell you." I tried to roll to my side, but he held me where I was, my body resting on his.

"Go ahead. Tell me. But I must be able to feel your comfort as you do."

"It's about Alejandro. I'm so sorry, Tres, but he's dead."

His eyes filled with tears before I'd even finished speaking his cousin's name. His mouth opened, but he didn't say a word. Didn't make a sound. Silent tears rolled down his cheeks. Tres could not have had a reaction that ripped my heart to shreds more than this.

I straddled him, lay my body against his, wrapped my arms around him, and held him as tightly as I could.

Finally, after what felt like an hour or more, Tres hugged me back and spoke. "He died protecting me, yes?"

"I believe so. I don't know the details of what happened, only what we've been able to piece together."

"Is that when you met Baltasar? After Alejandro's death?"

"Yes. I was there when he was informed."

"How did he react?"

I sighed. "As a man who'd just been told his son was dead."

"Why were you there?"

"So when you asked, I could tell you how he reacted."

He put his finger on my chin and tilted my head like he had before. "You mean that, don't you?"

"I do, Tres."

He hugged me tighter. "I thank God in heaven for bringing you to me."

I hugged him back. "I'm equally thankful he brought me you." I bit my lip, not sure now was the time to ask, but I did anyway. "Do you believe Baltasar was behind your kidnapping?"

Tres let out a deep breath. "I'm not certain. It was either him or my father, but neither makes sense." He shifted me off him. "I am sorry, *mi amor*, but…" He motioned with his head toward the bathroom.

I got out of bed, padded into the suite's main room, and when I didn't see a coffeemaker right away, I picked up the phone and ordered a pot along with cream, pastries, and fruit. When Tres joined me, naked like I was, I imagined our life just like this. Comfortable. As much in sync as we were in love.

"What are you thinking, *mi tormenta*?"

"How much I love being with you. How easy it feels."

"I am sorry I didn't tell you about my family."

"It hurt a lot at first, but then your mother said you'd told her about me, about us. That you planned to bring me to Mallorca to meet them. Then I felt better." I watched Tres' expression change with each word I spoke. He appeared to go from relaxed to puzzled to angry. "What?" I asked.

"Nothing." He shook his head and returned to the bedroom. When I followed, I was disappointed to see he'd put a robe on.

"Tres?"

"It's nothing." My heart sank when he didn't even turn around to look at me.

"Would you like to know what I thought when I met your parents?" I came across as angry too, because

I was. Also like him, I grabbed the hotel robe from the closet and wrapped myself in it, irritated that the sleeves were so long I had to roll them up, and once I had, they wouldn't stay that way.

"What are you doing?" Tres asked, putting his hand on one of mine.

"Nothing," I snapped.

He took a step back. "What is wrong?"

"Nothing," I repeated, giving up on the sleeves.

"Ellison?"

I walked out of the bedroom when I heard a knock at the door. Before I could open it, Tres moved me out of the way.

"Who is there?" he asked.

"El servicio de habitación, señor."

"Did you call for room service?"

I folded my arms. "I wanted coffee."

He put his finger in front of his lips and waved his hand for me to back away from the door.

"What?" I mouthed.

He went into the bedroom and came out with a gun.

"Tres? It's room service."

He stood up against the wall so when the door opened, the man wouldn't be able to see him.

"Please leave it," I said through the door.

"Sí, señora."

I watched through the peephole until the elevator doors closed with the man inside.

"Can I open it now?" I asked.

His eyes bored into mine. "Do you think I'm crazy?"

"Tres, please put down the gun."

He walked over and set it on a table near the sofa. Once he had, I took both his hands in mine. "No, I don't think you're crazy. I think you've just gone through a terrible ordeal and you're cautious. I understand."

"But?"

I shook my head. "No buts. I once told you that before I became an attorney, I worked for the CIA. I wasn't a secretary in an office, Tres. I was an agent. I executed missions. Dangerous ones. The most important thing I learned during my tenure with the agency is to trust my gut. If you don't feel safe, trust your instincts. I'll trust them too."

"You are formidable."

I didn't care for the look on his face but vowed to give him the benefit of the doubt. "What I am, is your wife."

"What happened? We went from loving each other so much to angry." He took a step closer so our bodies touched, and squeezed my hands.

"You shut me out."

His eyes scrunched.

"Don't pretend you don't know what I'm talking about." I tried to remove my hands from his, but he held tight. "When I told you your mother said you wanted to bring me to Mallorca. It triggered something, and you shut me out."

Tres closed his eyes, raised his face to the ceiling for a moment, then looked down at me. "I am sorry, Ellison."

"Tell me why."

He sighed. "I fear it will upset you more."

"*Not* telling me things will upset me more."

He pulled me over to the sofa. We both sat down, but he didn't release my hands. He took a deep breath. "I didn't tell her about you."

My head cocked. "What?"

"I did not talk to my mother about you."

"How did she know who I was? That we were married?"

"I can only assume Alejandro told her."

"I don't understand. She said so many things. She made me feel better about us."

"And perhaps that is all she wanted to do. It probably would not have comforted you if she had said, 'My nephew said my son married you.'"

"It certainly wouldn't have." I tried to pull my hand away, but Tres wouldn't let go. "Seriously? I *need* my coffee."

He hesitated for a moment, then stood, walked past the table where he'd set the gun, and over to the door. He picked up the tray that had been left outside, kicked the door closed with his foot, and brought it over and set it in front of me. He poured a cup, then added two teaspoons of sugar and a little cream before handing it to me.

"Thank you." I took a sip and rested against the sofa.

"You asked if I wanted to know what you thought when you met my parents."

"You remember that, huh?"

He smiled. "I may be a *bastardo* like my father, at times, but I will endeavor not to be very often."

"They keep things from each other."

Tres nodded. "You are right."

"It seemed like your father didn't know you were missing, and then it seemed like she didn't want him to know. I couldn't understand it."

"Perhaps she thought he was behind it."

"I thought that too. But God, Tres, that makes it even worse."

"It does."

"I don't want to live like they do. I don't want our marriage to be like theirs."

"Neither do I."

I took another sip of coffee, then set the cup on the table. "It isn't just that I don't want it. I won't do it, Tres. I can't."

He set the cup he held down like I had. "I understand, Ellison."

I raised a brow.

"I am sincere," he began. "I cannot promise you I'll be perfect—"

"I don't expect you to be."

"Thank you, but please let me finish."

My cheeks flushed. "I'm sorry I interrupted. Please continue."

"When I am a *bastardo*, do what you did today."

"Which thing I did?"

He smiled. "Do not let me get away with it. Tell me when I anger you. Tell me why."

"And you'll just accept it?"

"You know me as I know you, my love. It may not be easy, but I know what it feels like to wonder if I'll ever hold you in my arms again. I don't want to feel that way again."

"I don't either."

He put his hands on the knot I'd tied in the robe's belt. "I liked it better when we were both naked."

"I will *always* like it better when we're both naked."

As Tres led me back to bed, part of me felt guilty, wondering again if anyone had told his mother he'd been found. But we needed this time together and alone more than he needed to go to her. And that's what he'd have to do if he wanted to confront his father in person.

"Wait," I said when he picked me up and set me on the bed.

He shook his head.

"Let me just tell Vex you don't want your parents to know yet. He has no way of knowing you want to tell your father in person."

It took him a few seconds, but then he nodded. "One message, and that is all. You are mine, Ellison, and right now, all that matters is that we are together."

"I agree, Tres."

I sent the message, then waited for a response, hoping it came quickly. I breathed a sigh of relief when it did.

Roger that, Vex's text read. When I held my phone so Tres could see the screen, he took it from my hand and threw it to the other side of the room.

"Now, *mi tormenta,* I need to make love again to my wife."

23

Tres

While Ellison slept, her back nestled against my front, I thought about the things she'd said about my parents. First, that my mother said I'd told her about Ellison and our marriage. I couldn't have. I didn't speak with her between the time I met my love and when I was abducted. Alejandro had, though. As he'd said, she'd told him my father was closing in on us.

Also, she said my mother hadn't told my father I was missing. There were logical reasons why she would not. However, that the two led such separate lives troubled me in the same way it troubled Ellison. I didn't want that for us any more than she did.

The state of their marriage was one of many reasons I refused to stay on in my role as CEO of the Santoval Group. Even before I was forced to step into the job, I hadn't wanted to. I'd always believed it was the reason my parents lived their lives as recluses.

When I left Mallorca, I hadn't intended to go to Las Vegas. My mother's family was from Lower Manhattan—the area north of Houston Street in New York City—and it was where she'd urged Alejandro and me to go. I decided, instead, to see what it felt like to live my life anonymously. Simply.

I'd acquired the home on Desert Sunset Drive, putting it in the name of an LLC I'd formed both for privacy and also to make it harder for my father to locate me. However, from the first night I spent there, it hadn't felt right. I'd gone from living behind one set of gates in Spain to living behind another set in America. On top of that, everything about Las Vegas disgusted me in the same way living in Manhattan would have.

It was the *mercado* outside Austin, Texas, the one I took Ellison to see, that drew me to that part of the country. I couldn't recall where I'd heard of it, but I did remember the pull I felt to visit.

I smiled, thinking about my cousin's reaction to the place. It was as if with every step Alejandro took, his foot landed in *mierda de perro*—dog shit.

"No puedes hablar en serio," he'd said as we walked through the market.

I'd laughed and told him I was very serious after he'd questioned if I was, especially when we'd met Rojo and Bunker over a few cervezas while listening to the live music the place was known for.

When they talked about their job as security for a bar farther on the outskirts of Austin, I was intrigued. The next night, we'd visited the Long Branch, and a week later, I applied for and accepted a job as a bouncer.

Alejandro was certain I'd lost my mind, but the longer I worked there, the more I doubted I could ever return to my way of life in Mallorca.

My doubt turned to certainty the first time I saw Ellison at the place the regulars referred to as the Branch. I immediately knew I wanted her. More, I had to have her. It took several weeks before an opportunity arose for me to introduce myself. From the moment I held her in my arms as we danced, I knew we would spend our lives together.

I smiled again, thinking of how she'd tried so hard to push me away. My stubborn wife had no idea she'd met her match in me. When she confessed her loneliness the first night we'd made love, I vowed to her and myself she'd never feel that way again.

Whether my doing or not, breaking my promise to her had devastated me. My abduction had helped me understand—at least in part—why my parents lived in reclusivity. I could not imagine the anguish I would feel if I had not done everything in my power to protect her or the children we'd have someday. However, there had to be a way of life between how I'd lived in Texas and the way my parents did in Mallorca.

As far as the kind of life my wife and I would lead, money had never and would never be something I had to worry about. While my father's family was rich beyond imagination, my mother's family was more so. I'd received what I believed then to be a modest inheritance from her family when I reached the age of eighteen. Straightaway, I began to invest it. I'd accumulated enough wealth to afford most anything I wanted, including the houses I'd purchased in America and my airplane.

Having my own money meant I was able to live a life free from dependence on my father—something that drove him crazier the older I got.

I tightened my arms around Ellison when she moved in her sleep, and shifted so my cock rested between the cheeks of her ass. Had it even been an hour since we'd last made love? I doubted it, and yet, the desire I felt for her was as strong as it had been from the moment we set foot in the hotel's penthouse.

I knew we'd have to leave when the new day dawned in a few short hours. While I wanted to spend eternity in bed with my wife, there were things I needed to take care of and things I needed to know before I could rest easy enough to do so.

It was equally important for me to determine who was responsible for my abduction as it was for me to find my cousin's killer. I didn't doubt they were one and the same, at least in terms of who had orchestrated both. I'd hold those who'd carried out the dirty work responsible too, but not in the same way I did the masterminds.

When Ellison moved her hips again, soft moans escaping from her lips as though she was dreaming of our lovemaking, I put my hands on her naked breasts and thrust my rigid cock into her already wet pussy. When I reached between her legs with one hand, circling her clit with my fingertip, she cried out, clenching me so hard within her heat, I came faster than I'd intended to but at the same time she did.

"What time is it?" she murmured over her shoulder.

"It is early, my love. Go back to sleep." Within a few minutes, if that long, I knew she had. For me, rest would not come so easily. My mind refused to stop racing. I doubted it would until I had every answer I sought.

Ellison knew as well as I did we'd leave Madrid today. She confirmed as much when she'd said that, while she'd prefer my naked body be at her disposal indefinitely, in order for us to step outside the hotel, we'd need to make arrangements for someone to bring something for me to wear.

"The guy you shot is going to pull through," Vex said when he dropped clothing off for me at our suite.

I nodded. While I wanted him and everyone else who'd held me captive to pay for doing so, I felt relieved no one's blood was on my hands.

"However, we haven't been able to get a straight answer about who he's working for."

"What do you mean by 'straight answer?'" Ellison asked.

"He insists he doesn't know."

Once we'd boarded the private aircraft that would take us to Mallorca, Vex confirmed their team had been able to keep the details of my whereabouts concealed. Not knowing where I was, had to be making whoever had orchestrated my kidnapping frantic. Which meant, once I came face-to-face with my father, I would immediately know if it had been him.

Given I had a way to access the estate and the house without him discovering I'd arrived on the property until I stood before him, he would have no time to mask his reaction.

When Alejandro and I were kids, we'd found it, aided by one of the sons of the household staff, and had made use of it throughout our teenage years.

Thinking of my cousin and our antics hurt worse than anything I'd experienced in my life. When Ellison confirmed my belief he'd died protecting me, the guilt I felt then and since would remain with me until the day I died as well.

Before leaving the hotel suite, Ellison and I had discussed my plan for confronting my father as well as Baltasar. Instead, now that we'd arrived outside the walls of my parents' compound, the plan we were about to execute was hers.

"Ready?" she asked as we stood on the shore of the Bay of Palma, about to scramble up the rocks and onto the Barello Estate.

"Give us a moment, *por favor*," I said to Vex and Kruger, who Ellison had insisted accompany us. More accurately, she'd insisted Vex, Kruger, and herself accompany me.

I gathered her in my arms and held her body close to mine. "There are so many things I want to say to you," I began when her gaze met mine. "'I love you' will never seem adequate to express how I feel. 'Thank you' will never convey how grateful I am you love me too."

She brushed my lips with hers. "Let's get this over with." My wife was beautiful, sexy, smart, and funny. She was also pragmatic. "The sooner we do, the sooner we can focus on the rest of our lives."

The trail my cousin and I had used to sneak in and out of my parents' home led to an unused service entrance—except by ourselves and the boy who'd first shown it to us. When we were younger, the close proximity of my father's study to it meant if he was home, we had to be diligent to either not come in that way or to be extra quiet when we did. Today, I did not care.

I'd asked Ellison to wait just outside the door with Vex and Kruger when I went inside. His chair was turned toward the outside window, and while I couldn't see his face, I knew it was him.

"Padre?" I said in a firm voice meant to startle him.

When he spun around, I saw he held a photo in his hand. Tears ran down his cheeks. Until today, I had never seen my father cry.

"Tres?" he said, looking up at me and blinking as though he'd seen a ghost. "Tres?" he repeated, getting up from his chair and rushing over to me. *"Mi hijo?"*

I could not remember the last time my father had embraced me. I stood, stunned, when that is what he did, holding me as tightly as I'd held Ellison in the alleyway in *Barrio de las Letras.*

"¿Estás vivo?"

"Sí, padre, estoy vivo."

When I assured him that, yes, I was alive, he rushed over to his desk and picked up the photo he'd been holding. It was of Alejandro and me when we were boys, probably around the same age as when we'd first discovered the way to sneak in and out of the house.

"Alejandro?" he asked.

I shook my head and told him I was sorry. *"Lo siento, papa."*

He leaned against his desk, let go of the photo, and it floated to the floor. I walked over, but rather than pick it up, I embraced him like he had me.

I felt a hand on my shoulder and turned my head to look into Ellison's eyes. "Papa, I'd like you to meet my wife," I said to him in English, which he spoke as fluently as I did.

I stepped back and watched as he looked from me to her, then back again.

"I did not know she was your wife."

As I'd told Ellison more than once, my father was a bastard. He was not, however, an actor. His reactions were authentic.

"Where is Mother?" I asked.

"I do not know."

When my eyes met Ellison's a second time, she nodded and excused herself.

"Tres?" I heard her say a few moments later. I stepped away from my father and walked over to the door where she stood.

"Your mother is on her way to Baltasar's house," she whispered.

My eyes opened wide in understanding.

"Papa, when did you learn of Alejandro's death?" I asked.

"Right before you came in. Perhaps ten minutes. I'm not sure. It is why I thought you were a ghost."

"I need to go, but I will come back and we'll talk."

When he nodded and hung his head in resignation, I realized how much my father had changed since the last time I saw him. Or had it been before that? He seemed more like an old man with drooping shoulders and dark circles under his eyes than the man I had been intimidated by most of my life.

"I will come back," I repeated. A feeling of sadness overwhelmed me when he didn't ask where I was going.

As Vex drove from our estate to my uncle's, I wondered if my father's health was worse than I'd been told. Maybe in the time since my abduction, he'd suffered another heart episode.

"That's your mother's car," said Ellison, pointing once we'd driven through the gate and up to the house.

I looked over at the vehicle parked at an angle. The driver's door had been left ajar. The front door to Baltasar's house was open as well.

I jumped out of the SUV and ran to it. "Where is my mother?" I shouted at the housekeeper standing near it.

She pointed. *"La terraza."*

I raced forward, halting when I saw my mother facing my uncle and holding a gun pointed at him.

"Where is Tres?" she screamed at him. I was about to step forward when I felt Ellison's hand on my arm.

"Let us," she whispered, motioning with her head at Vex and Kruger.

"Mrs. Barello—Amanda—I need you to drop the gun," she said in a loud but calm voice.

My mother didn't flinch. "Not until he tells me what he's done with my son."

Baltasar's hands were in the air, and when his eyes met mine, he shook his head almost imperceptibly.

"He was with Alejandro, and you killed him!" she screamed. "Tell me what you've done with my son. I kept him safe from you, but you killed him. *Just like you killed your own son.*"

Ellison turned to me and nodded.

"Mama, I am here."

The gun fell from my mother's hands, she turned around, and raced toward me. I didn't see the same relief in her eyes as I had seen in my father's. Instead, I saw desperation, perhaps even madness. I took a step back and put my hands out in front of me.

"Tres?" she cried.

"What have you done?" I said without thinking, yet knowing—somehow—she had.

She stood in front of me, her eyes now beseeching. "I kept you safe, Tres. You and Alejandro." She pointed at my uncle. "From him! *He was going to kill you.*"

"I don't understand. I am fine." I waved my hands in front of my body.

"Only because I protected you."

"Come, Amanda," said Ellison, taking my mother's arm. "Let's go home, and you can tell us what happened."

"Wait," I heard my uncle shout when I turned to follow my wife and my mother out to the car.

I stood where I was, waiting as he approached with Kruger. Vex rushed ahead of them. "He says he wants to talk about Alejandro."

I studied him. "What should I do?"

"We can handle it if you'd prefer."

"No. I need to hear what he has to say."

Vex nodded. "I'll go wait with Fury and your mother."

My uncle slowly walked toward me. Had he been a child, it would have looked as though he was dragging his feet. Except he wasn't a child, and like my father, he appeared to have aged many years since I last saw him. Also like my father, his once-square shoulders drooped and the dark circles beneath his eyes made them look hollow.

When he reached the part of the terrace where I stood, he motioned to the chair. When I nodded, he sat, leaned forward, and put his head in his hands.

"When does this end, *Tío*?"

He raised his head and looked into my eyes. "It is finished, *sobrino*."

"Was it you? Did you kill Alejandro?"

"You think I would kill my own son? My own flesh and blood?"

"Did my mother lie? We share blood too, Baltasar. Didn't you intend to kill me?"

I saw pain in his eyes, but not denial.

"Who, Baltasar? Tell me now, or I'll have you taken into custody."

My eyes filled with tears, hearing my uncle's cry of anguish as he covered his face with his hands. "I cannot," he wailed. *"I cannot."*

"You must. You must end this."

"You would have me lose two sons? Was one not enough?"

He could not see me, but I nodded, knowing exactly who had killed Alejandro when he said "two sons." "You cannot protect Pascual, Baltasar."

He shook his head too violently, and when he looked up at me, I saw the same desperation, the same madness as had been in my mother's eyes. "It…it… wasn't Pascual. It was me." He held out his hands. "Arrest me."

"And what if he kills again? Next time, will it be Eliana? Raymon? Orlando?" I closed my eyes and turned my face to the sun, cursing the business that had all but destroyed our family. I walked closer and squeezed his shoulder, first in comfort, then more tightly, intending to cause pain. "Where is he?" When he didn't answer quickly enough, I grabbed his arm and pulled him to his feet. *"Where is Pascual?"* I shouted into his face.

"In Madrid."

"Where?" I repeated, gripping his arm even tighter.

"Gregorio Marañón Hospital."

I turned around when I heard footsteps and saw two local *policía* approaching with Kruger.

"We'll take care of things here," he said. "You go with Ellison and your mother."

24

Fury

While Vex, Amanda, and I waited for Tres to join us, his mother rambled on and on, insisting her only agenda had been to protect her son.

"Baltasar was going to kill him," she cried. "That's why he had to leave Mallorca. Alejandro too."

I couldn't glean whether Tres and his father had actually had the argument she told me about the night I first met her, but whether it took place or not, she'd managed to convince him Leandro had duped him into taking the job as CEO of Santoval.

"When Alejandro informed me you and Tres had married and he planned to bring you to Mallorca to meet us, I knew I couldn't allow that to happen—Baltasar would've killed him the minute he set foot in Spain. I had to stop him."

"By kidnapping him?"

"It was the only way. Alejandro and I both knew that if we told Tres the truth, he'd never agree to remain in hiding. He'd confront his uncle."

"Are you saying Alejandro was in on it?"

"He said he'd make the arrangements. Tres was to be kept in hiding but safe. The last I heard from him was when the plane left Houston. When I learned Alejandro was dead…I thought Baltasar had killed my Tres too."

"What made you think your brother-in-law intended to kill Tres?"

"Eliana overheard him and Pascual talking about it."

I remembered she was Alejandro's next oldest sibling, yet as a woman, would not be permitted to take over as CEO of Santoval.

"She was helping Alejandro and me gather evidence against her father and brother. Once we had enough for them to be arrested, the plan was to let Tres go."

I shook my head. As if it ever would've been that simple. I heard sirens, looked up, and saw two police vehicles pull through the gates. Vex ushered Amanda into the backseat of the SUV as they raced into the house.

"What's happening?" she asked.

"I don't know," I responded, then turned to Vex. "You good?" I asked.

"I'll stay with Amanda," he said, motioning toward the front door. "Tres is headed this way now."

I raced up the steps and into his arms.

"It was Pascual. He killed Alejandro," he said, resting his head on my shoulder. I could feel the dampness of his tears.

"I'm so sorry, Tres."

"My mother…Some things she said…" He shook his head. "I'm not sure I want to know, or that I can begin to understand."

"Let's get her back to the house."

We were walking toward the SUV when Kruger came out the front door followed by the two policemen and Tres' uncle.

"What's happening?" I asked.

"They're taking him in for questioning."

"He is in a hell of his own making," Tres mumbled as we watched Baltasar being led away in handcuffs.

"Rile is on his way here now," Kruger added. "He and I will go to Madrid and question Pascual. By the way, while he suffered a gunshot wound requiring surgery, it wasn't life-threatening. The police are already at the hospital. "

I sat in the back with Amanda while Vex drove to the Barello Estate. From where he sat in the front passenger seat, I could see the pain and anguish etched on Tres' face. I wished I could spare him the ordeal of having to listen to the truth of what his mother had done, but I couldn't. He had to hear it for himself, process it for himself. Once he'd gone through as much as he could bear tonight, I would be there to give him comfort and ease his pain as best I could.

Tomorrow, we would begin again—learning things we hadn't yet and making decisions about our future. While this wasn't the time for us to discuss it, I had already decided to resign my position as counsel for the Invincibles. My husband needed me more than they did. Hammer had found me; he would eventually find another attorney. In the interim, he could manage it in the same way he had for years.

When we pulled up to the house and parked, Vex got out, came around, and led Amanda inside. Tres and I walked up the steps, but before we went inside, he opened his arms, and I fell into his embrace. We remained that way, holding each other tightly for several minutes.

"You are about to say we should get this over with," he said when I started to pull back.

"Not this time," I told him. "If there was any way we could avoid the conversation we're about to have, I would."

"You will be with me, Ellison."

He hadn't phrased it as a question, but I responded as if he had. "I will always be with you, Tres. I'm your wife."

He looked into my eyes. "Do you think she was behind it?"

"I know she was. She confessed that she and Alejandro had reason to believe Baltasar and Pascual were plotting to kill you. Apparently, Eliana overheard them discussing it. Anyway, that's where it all began. First, getting you to go to America, then kidnapping you when they thought you intended to return to Mallorca to introduce me to your family."

"She and Alejandro?"

"I'm sorry, Tres, but from what she said, he was involved."

"They thought they were protecting me." Again, he hadn't phrased it as a question.

I held him tighter. "I believe that was their intention."

"Do you think my father was involved?"

I cupped his cheek. "I don't."

"He is not well."

"He didn't seem to be."

"And Baltasar…I cannot imagine how tortured his soul must be."

"He lost his son."

"He lost two," said Tres, his eyes filling with tears. "All for money and power." He gripped the back of my neck, and the pain I saw on his face turned to anger. "I don't want it. Do you understand? I want no part of Santoval."

"Neither do I."

He closed his eyes and raised his face to the sky.

"We should go inside."

He looked down at me. "I know, but I don't want to."

When we walked in, I was stunned to see Kensington sitting in the solarium with Amanda and Scottie. She stood and met us in the foyer.

"Rile and I knew you'd all need support."

"Thank you," I said, squeezing her hand. "Tres, this is Rile's wife, Kensington. Kensington, please meet my husband."

"Have you seen my father?" he asked.

"The last I knew, he was with Vex in his study."

He'd taken one step in that direction when I heard Vex shout for help. Tres and I rushed in.

"Call for an ambulance," he said between breaths as he performed CPR on Leandro. I knelt down to help when I saw Tres calling.

"Ready?" Vex asked after he'd completed a set of compressions and breaths.

I took over, and after I'd done the same, we switched again. By then, we could hear the ambulance arriving.

"Possible heart attack," I heard him explain as I stood, walked over to Tres, and put my hand in his.

"I must go with him," he said. "But what about my mother?"

Scottie was waiting outside the door when Tres and I followed the paramedics and his father from the room.

"Please remain with Amanda," I said to her.

"Of course."

I looked over at Vex. "You stay too. Do not let her leave the house."

"Understood," he said, nodding. "Do you want someone to drive you to the hospital?"

"Pedro is here," Kensington said from the other room.

By the time we got to the front door, a helicopter was landing on the front lawn. Tres and I watched as his father was carried over and his stretcher loaded on.

"Come, we'll meet them there," I said to Tres, leading him to where Pedro waited.

We stayed at the hospital for several hours after learning Leandro required bypass surgery. On more than one occasion, Tres insisted I go get some rest, but I refused to leave his side.

Once his father was out of recovery, stable, and in a room on the cardiac care floor, we left the hospital and returned to the Barello Estate. Given it was shortly before dawn, I doubted anyone would be awake. However, Scottie greeted us as we came in the front door.

"How's Amanda?" I asked.

"Distraught and worried, but her mania seemed to subside as the night went on. She took a sedative around midnight, and we expect her to sleep for a few more hours." She looked over at Tres. "How's your father?"

"He made it through surgery and is now recovering," he said, scrubbing his face with his hand.

"The two of you look exhausted. Everything is under control here, so I encourage you to get some rest."

"Is Vex here?" I asked.

"He's lying down right now, but here."

I knew I should ask if she'd heard an update from Rile or Kruger about Pascual, but Tres looked like he'd fall over from exhaustion if he didn't sleep soon. There'd be time later to sort through more than just what had happened with his cousin.

"Do you want to stay here?" I asked him.

"I need you with me, Ellison."

I put my arm around him and guided him to the staircase. "That's nonnegotiable, husband. I will remain by your side forever."

I saw a glimmer of a smile cross his face.

We both slept restlessly in Tres' old room until shortly after noon. Even after we'd woken up, we remained in bed.

"I am at a loss for words this morning, my love," Tres said, turning to his side. I did the same, and he cupped my cheek.

"You shouldn't feel as though you need to talk right now, Tres."

"It is more that I don't know how to thank you for all you've done."

"I'm your wife. We'll navigate this life together, facing its challenges, working to overcome them, and celebrating the happy times."

"*Eres un milagro*—a miracle."

"Our love is a miracle."

Tres leaned forward and brushed my lips with his.

"When would you like to return to the hospital?" I asked.

"Soon, but first, I need to talk to my mother."

I nodded, but Tres shook his head.

"What?" I asked.

"I misspoke. *We* need to talk to my mother."

I smiled. "If you'd prefer to speak to her alone, I'll understand."

Tres rolled to his back. "I'd prefer not to speak to her at all."

"I understand that too."

"She is responsible for Alejandro's death."

"Indirectly." I sighed. "She will torture herself over it for the rest of her life."

Tres' eyes drifted closed, and for a minute, I thought he'd gone back to sleep. I knew he hadn't when I saw tears roll down his cheeks.

I wrapped my arm around him and held as tightly as I could, wishing I could ease his pain.

Finally, he took a deep breath and turned to his side. "It isn't just talking with my mother. There is so much for us to talk about today too. So much to figure out. Our entire future, yes?"

"Yes. I came to a decision yesterday, Tres. I'm going to resign as attorney of record for the Invincibles."

"No!" he gasped, his eyes wide. "You cannot. I will not let you."

I raised a brow.

"Let me rephrase. I will encourage you not to."

"You'll need to remain in Spain, and if I have learned anything in these last few days, it's that I can't live without you. If you're here, I will be too."

"Yes, I will need to stay for some time, primarily due to my father's health, but I do not intend to be in Mallorca longer than is absolutely necessary."

"But—"

Tres put his fingertips on my lips. "Our life together is in America, *mi tormenta*. There is nothing for me in Mallorca."

"Your family and your family's business is here."

"We will visit my family. As for Santoval, it is no longer my concern. I have resigned as CEO, and in the next few days, I will also resign from the board."

There was no reason for me to argue with Tres about this now. There was no telling what would happen today, tomorrow, and in the days to follow.

Epilogue

Tres

My father's surgery was to bypass the parts of his heart no longer working effectively. Instead, it seemed more as though the whole thing had been transplanted. Perhaps facing mortality, as he did, had made him reconsider the way he'd lived his life. Then again, maybe it wasn't just his near brush with death but everything that had happened in the last few months.

He and I grew close during his recovery in ways I never imagined possible, and I got to know the man I'd once considered my nemesis.

I felt Alejandro's loss profoundly, but having Ellison by my side made it bearable. The sadness and regret weren't diminished, but having her comfort is what got me through each day.

It wasn't easy for me to lean on her. However, when she felt I was "shutting her out," she was quick to remind me not to.

My mother had fallen into a deep depression and had been hospitalized for several days when we worried her mental state might cause her to harm herself.

Regardless of the turmoil she was experiencing, it was difficult for me to be anything but honest with her about my feelings. Part of me did blame her for Alejandro's death, but more, I was angry about her lies and manipulation.

When Ellison had shared the story my mother told her the first night they met, I was furious. My father and I had not argued, nor had he threatened to disown or disinherit me. Instead, it had been my mother who spun a lie in order to get me to leave the country by saying my father had no plans to return as CEO of Santoval.

While her role in my kidnapping was not revealed to anyone outside our immediate family and the men and women Ellison worked for, our relationship remained strained. No matter how many times she pleaded with me to understand what she'd done was for my protection, my response was the same. Had she been honest with me, Alejandro might still be alive. I knew my words hurt, but she needed to hear them if she wanted any kind of relationship with me in the future.

I wouldn't have traded my cousin's life for any-thing. However, I knew if my mother had not butted in and convinced me to go to America, I may never have met *mi tormenta*. It was hardly a consolation, though.

As far as what had happened in the hangar in Madrid, Pascual was arrested for the murder of his brother. During questioning, he told the police one of the men Alejandro had hired to help with my kidnapping was really working for him. That was how he knew when and where the plane would arrive and that I was on it. And, as I'd thought when I first heard my cousin and closest friend was dead, according to Pascual, Alejandro had died protecting me.

My uncle was also arrested, but for conspiracy to commit murder after his daughter Eliana delivered enough evidence for the police to press charges. While I had no doubt Baltasar would experience a torment of his own making for the rest of his life over the death of his oldest son, he deserved to be behind bars in the same way Pascual did.

The relationship between my parents remained ten-uous, but in the same way my father had made an effort to mend our relationship, I knew he would eventually do the same with her. I did not confide in him that I hadn't yet forgiven her for all she'd done. That was between my mother and me. I knew I would, in time, especially with my Ellison by my side, reminding me what was important in life. *Love above all else.*

Perhaps in honor of Alejandro, the dream he and I had shared to change the rules of succession within Santoval came to fruition. From now on, the board of directors would be responsible for naming current and future CEOs.

I felt his presence the day Eliana was given the official title and all the responsibility running the family business entailed. What I hadn't expected, was the smile I saw on my father's face when the board announced publicly she would be the first female CEO to serve in that capacity.

"I'm surprised you are in favor of her appointment," I said to him as we were leaving.

"If it weren't for Eliana, you might not be here. If I'd had to choose between having my son in my life or having a woman take over Santoval, the decision would be easy."

I convinced Ellison not to resign her position, joking we would need her income if she wouldn't let me return to my job as bouncer at the Long Branch. The truth was, we didn't need the money and never would. My reason for wanting her to remain as legal counsel for the Invincibles was because I'd seen the satisfaction performing the job brought her.

We'd traveled home to Texas several times and returned to Mallorca when we were needed. And while God hadn't blessed us with any children yet, we practiced making them every day and night. We also practiced parenting skills when her niece and nephew came to spend the night with us or when we took them on outings to give Stephanie and Jimmy time for things like dates. Ellison's sister promised to return the favor when our little ones came along.

While we'd been in Mallorca for the last few days, today we were returning to America to celebrate the Thanksgiving holiday with Ellison's family.

In December, once my father was cleared to travel, Hammer and Maeve had offered to host a celebration at the Long Branch similar to the one that took place the night Ellison and I first spent in each other's arms. This time, among other things, we would be celebrating our marriage.

According to Rile, everyone would be in attendance, including those on the team who were based in Europe and other parts of the United States. When he said it wouldn't be limited to partners and that contractors' attendance was *required* as well, Ellison had raised a brow.

"God, I hope the Invincibles partners aren't all planning to retire like Hammer did," she'd whispered.

"To each, a happy life to live," I'd said in response. Few words meant as much to me as those did. When the time came we were blessed with children, my wife and I agreed they would be free to make their own decisions about the life they wanted to lead. Whether it was to become attorneys like their mother, CIA agents like she had been, or even bouncers at a bar, we would respect their choice.

"Remember, Tres, that includes running Santoval one day," she said when we'd last discussed it.

I'd chuckled, but if that was the choice one or more of our children made, I would be proud.

An hour into the flight, Ellison sighed and rested her head on my shoulder.

"What is troubling you, *mi tormenta*?" I asked.

"Decker and Rile are insisting Vex and I name the new team." It had filled my heart with pride when Ellison told me she and Vex had been named managing partners.

"What have you come up with so far?" I asked.

"Nothing," she groaned in frustration.

I looked across the aisle and saw Vex was asleep. Scottie's head rested on his shoulder.

"I'm sure the two of you will come up with something."

Kruger, who was seated in a row in front of us, stood. "I have an idea."

"Thank God. What is it?" she asked.

"It's something you said when we were looking for Tres."

Ellison turned to me with a puzzled expression, then back to him. "I don't remember."

"You said, 'We aren't going to stop until we find him.'"

"Okay…"

"How about the Unstoppables? We won't stop until the mission is complete."

Vex raised his head. "I like it."

"Do you think Decker will go for it?" Kruger asked.

"It isn't his decision. It's ours," said Vex. "Besides, with a name as bad as the Invincibles, the original partners have no room to criticize our choice."

"What do you think, my love?"

She looked at Kruger, then at Vex. "It's settled. We are officially the Unstoppable Intelligence and Security Group."

Keep reading for a sneak peek at the
next book in
Heather Slade's Unstoppables
Team One Series,
Vexed

1

Vex

Spending Christmas at home. Talk next year.

I reread the message I'd received from McKenna "Scottie" Walsh, aka the woman I *thought* I was in a relationship with. The same woman whose bed I'd rolled out of this morning, promising I'd call after the meeting I had scheduled with Fury, my partner in the Unstoppables, the new Invincibles team.

Scottie hadn't mentioned being gone for Christmas then or last night, or any of the five nights before when we fell asleep in each other's arms.

"Are you okay?" asked Fury.

"Yeah. Uh, sorry. Let's get started."

She leaned against the back of her chair. "You're distracted. Tell me what's going on, or there's no point in even having this meeting."

If anyone besides Fury had spoken those same words to me, I would have assured them I was, in fact, paying attention and asked them to get started. She knew me too well for me to get away with such bullshit. We'd worked together on several assignments before she quit the agency and got her law degree. The mutual respect between us was strong. In fact, we often joked we were more like siblings than coworkers.

"Scottie is spending Christmas at home. Without me," I confessed, holding up my phone. "This is how she told me."

"Did you just receive her message?"

I nodded.

"Odd."

"I'll say." I had no doubt Fury knew Scottie and I were seeing each other, but she might not know how seriously. "We've been together every night since we returned from Spain last month. She spent Thanksgiving with our family."

"Have you talked about Christmas?"

"Indirectly."

Fury raised a brow. "What does that mean?"

"We didn't talk about spending it apart."

This time, she rolled her eyes. "I'm sorry to hear she won't be at the party this weekend."

I was too. Decker Ashford and Rile DeLéon had organized a joint Invincibles and Unstoppables Christmas party. Not only were we celebrating the holidays, but it marked the first time all the partners of both units, as well as the employees and contractors, would be gathered together in one place. Attendance was mandatory, barring an emergency, either for one of the guests personally or a mission.

Since Scottie worked for the FBI rather than either firm, I'd invited her as my plus one. "That's another thing," I muttered.

"What?" she asked.

"She was supposed to be my date for the party. 'Talk next year' sure makes it sounds like she won't be."

"Are you sure you didn't have some kind of disagreement?"

It was my turn to roll my eyes. "You may think I'm a Neanderthal, but I think I would know if we'd had a disagreement."

"How did you leave things with her?"

I raised a brow, also like she had a few minutes ago. "You sure you want to hear the details?"

Fury closed her eyes and plugged her ears. "No! I definitely do not. I won't be able to unhear whatever it is."

"So, yeah. Not a disagreement."

The calls I'd made and texts I'd sent to Scottie over the next two days had all gone unanswered. If the party tonight hadn't been mandatory, I certainly would've been a no-show. Instead, my also-dateless brother and I went together.

"Can you at least try to have a good time?" he asked when we walked into the Long Branch, where the festivities were taking place.

"Fuck off," I muttered, walking over to the bar to order a drink.

"Everything's on the house tonight, sir," said one of the special-event bartenders the owners had brought in just for this occasion. When I slapped a buck on the bar for a tip, he slid it back to me. "Tipping's not allowed either."

I shoved the money in my pocket, leaned my back against the bar, and took in the crowded scene. While I recognized almost everyone here, there were a few I didn't. Most appeared to be either spouses or dates of team members, but some were probably contractors I hadn't met yet. Not that I was in the mood to meet new people.

"There he is," I heard Tres, Fury's husband, say. "Looking as grouchy as my wife warned me you'd be."

"Let him be. You'd be grouchy too if I wasn't here," said Fury to Tres before reaching up to kiss my cheek. "Have you heard from Scottie?"

I shook my head. "Not a word."

Fury's eyes scrunched. "Something's up. Have you tried calling?"

"Only about once an hour. I've even considered catching a flight out tomorrow and confronting her in person."

"That's what I'd do," said Tres as he nuzzled Fury's neck. I was about to suggest they either get a room or, at least, go dance when my cell vibrated.

I pulled it out of my pocket and swiped the screen. "It's a message from Scottie."

"Is everything okay?"

I looked up from the phone and shook my head. "It says she's been arrested."

About the Author

USA Today and Amazon Top 15 Bestselling Author Heather Slade writes shamelessly sexy, edge-of-your seat romantic suspense.

She gave herself the gift of writing a book for her own birthday one year. Forty-plus books later (and counting), she's having the time of her life.

The women Slade writes are self-confident, strong, with wills of their own, and hearts as big as the Colorado sky. The men are sublimely sexy, seductive alphas who rise to the challenge of capturing the sweet soul of a woman whose heart they'll hold in the palm of their hand forever. Add in a couple of neck-snapping twists and turns, a page-turning mystery, and a swoon-worthy HEA, and you'll be holding one of her books in your hands.

She loves to hear from my readers. You can contact her at heather@heatherslade.com

To keep up with her latest news and releases, please visit her website at www.heatherslade.com to sign up for her newsletter.

MORE FROM AUTHOR HEATHER SLADE

BUTLER RANCH
Kade's Worth
Brodie's Promise
Maddox's Truce
Naughton's Secret
Mercer's Vow
Kade's Return
Butler Ranch Christmas

WICKED WINEMAKERS
FIRST LABEL
Brix's Bid
Ridge's Release
Press' Passion
Zin's Sins
Tryst's Temptation

WICKED WINEMAKERS
SECOND LABEL
Beau's Beloved
Coming Soon:
Cru's Crush
Bones' Bliss
Snapper's Seduction
Kick's Kiss

ROARING FORK RANCH
Coming Soon:
Roaring Fork Wrangler
Roaring Fork Roughstock
Roaring Fork Rockstar
Roaring Fork Rooker
Roaring Fork Bridger

THE ROYAL AGENTS
OF MI6
Make Me Shiver
Drive Me Wilder
Feel My Pinch
Chase My Shadow
Find My Angel

K19 SECURITY
SOLUTIONS TEAM ONE
Razor's Edge
Gunner's Redemption
Mistletoe's Magic
Mantis' Desire
Dutch's Salvation

K19 SECURITY
SOLUTIONS TEAM TWO
Striker's Choice
Monk's Fire
Halo's Oath
Tackle's Honor
Onyx's Awakening

K19 SHADOW OPERATIONS
TEAM ONE
Code Name: Ranger
Code Name: Diesel
Code Name: Wasp
Code Name: Cowboy
Code Name: Mayhem

K19 ALLIED INTELLIGENCE
TEAM ONE
Code Name: Ares
Code Name: Cayman
Code Name: Poseidon
Code Name: Zeppelin
Code Name: Magnet

K19 ALLIED INTELLIGENCE
TEAM TWO
Coming Soon:
Code Name: Puck
Code Name: Michelangelo
Code Name: Typhon
Code Name: Hornet
Code Name: Reaper

PROTECTORS
UNDERCOVER
Undercover Agent
Undercover Emissary
Coming Soon:
Undercover Savior
Undercover Infidel
Undercover Assassin

THE INVINCIBLES
TEAM ONE
Decked
Edged
Grinded
Riled
Smoked

THE INVINCIBLES
TEAM TWO
Bucked
Irished
Sainted
Hammered
Ripped

THE UNSTOPPABLES
TEAM ONE
Furied
Merried

COWBOYS OF
CRESTED BUTTE
A Cowboy Falls
A Cowboy's Dance
A Cowboy's Kiss
A Cowboy Stays
A Cowboy Wins